THE BIG FIX

Ever restless, ROGER L. SIMON has spent his life moving between books and movies, gaining distinction in both. In books, he is best known for the seven Moses Wine detective novels, which have won prizes in the U.S. and Great Britain and been published in over a dozen languages. In film, most prominent among his six produced screenplays—including his adaptation of *The Big Fix*—is *Enemies, A Love Story*, for which Simon was nominated for an Academy Award. Recently, he has turned to directing, filming the independent *Prague Duet*, which he co-wrote with his wife, Sheryl Longin, and which was a Romance Classics Premiere in 1999. He lives in Los Angeles, California.

D0989275

THE BIG FIX

ROGER L. SIMON

ibooks
new york
www.ibooksinc.com

DISTRIBUTED BY SIMON & SCHUSTER, INC

An Original Publication of ibooks, inc.

Pocket Books, a division of Simon & Schuster, Inc.
1230 Avenue of the Americas, New York, NY 10020

An ibooks, inc. Book

ibooks, inc.
24 West 25th Street
New York, NY 10010

The ibooks World Wide Web Site Address is:
http://www.ibooksinc.com

ISBN 0-671-03906-7
First Pocket Books printing March 2000
10 9 8 7 6 5 4 3 2 1
POCKET and colophon are registered trademarks of Simon & Schuster, Inc.

Cover design by Jason Vita
Cover art © James Rosenquist / Licensed by VAGA, New York, NY
Interior design by Michael Mendelsohn at MM Design 2000, Inc.

Printed in the U.S.A.

For
Lance Richbourg,
In the American Grain

Richard Dreyfuss as Moses Wine
in the 1978 production of The Big Fix.

INTRODUCTION

by

RICHARD DREYFUSS

The '60s have taken a beating, haven't they?

And it's not just George Will and Patrick Buchanan. Oh no, throw a rock in any direction and you hit someone making fun, criticizing, shaking their heads in collective disapproval—of what? A *decade,* fuhcrissake! Get a life, people! Leave my '60s alone.

There, I said it: *My '60s.* I said it, and I'm glad.

Not the tasteless '70s, with everyone looking like barbers in Flatbush, or the cheery, sensitive '80s, with their GETOUTOFMYWAYYOULOSER serenity. And, need it be said, not the '90s, with their ever plummeting level of crassness and smallness of spirit. With all its bad rep, the '60s were the last gasp of principle and passion that we've had in this sorry excuse for a century.

Yeah, drugs. Bad. Definitely bad, no argument. Yeah, naiveté, in spades, and personally, I think the tie-die thing was silly. But ending a bad war was a good thing, and you can revise history all you want, but that happened, and we did it, and I'll always be proud of it. It was a real Frank Capra moment, big and important and dangerous.

It's fashionable today to scorn the values held up in the '60s, but we were experimenting with a lot of things, not just drugs. We thought for a moment that we and the world could handle a lot more love, and many of us tried to practice it. We thought that America—the America we learned about in 7th and 8th grade history classes, where the propaganda was effective and we all fell in love with our country—could be a real part of our lives. There certainly wasn't a lot of support for the effort, and it did go awry sometimes, but not always, not always . . .

They say (and it was the '60s generation who was the first to point a finger at Them) that we were irresponsibly tearing things down in those days—the country, the family, the ties that bound . . .

Bullshit.

We were building up America, asking that it reflect what it had said it was, asking the nation to reflect what it talked about on the 4th of July.

If you wanted to put words to the '60s, one of those words would have to be "learning." Some people—mostly young, but not always—learned some profound things, in beds, in homes, in the streets, even, God help us, in their drugged-out brains.

Moses Wine knew this. Moses was a Shamus. Remember how all the great detectives had a code, a lonely code? Well, Moses' code was based in the '60s, and he was alone with it, and a knight errant, just the same. He survived the '60s, and probably felt guilty about that, and he took into the rest of his life the feelings of nobility reached for, and honor, and love of Country, and he hid them behind his cynical armor and took them out only when he was alone or with his kids. And Roger Simon knew that, and wrote better about it than just about anyone, hiding his affection and regard and insights under the guise of a simple detective series.

I loved playing Moses Wine, and I will always regret that we couldn't make one or two or ten sequels. I would have loved making a fortune playing him, and I would have loved playing him for his rightness of character. I would have loved giving Roger that gift, but, like we learned in the '60s and every other decade I'm aware of, Life Is Not Fair. As it is, Roger can know that he got "It" right, and I don't think anyone else really has—not all the Bill Bennett tyoes, with all his scrutiny and moralizing.

The '60s were not a time of license and riot; not really. They were our Spanish Civil War, our test, our moment where our reach for something fine exceeded our grasp.

But reach we did, and we haven't reached at all, since, to our collective shame.

Richard Dreyfuss
Los Angeles, CA

THE
BIG FIX

1

THE LAST TIME I was with Lila Shea we were making love in the back of a 1952 Chrysler hearse parked across the street from the Oakland Induction Center. Tear gas was seeping through the floorboards and the crack of police truncheons was in our ears. I could barely hear her little cries over the wail of sirens. That was the fall of '67 — the October Days of Protest—and just a few moments after we finished, she bounced off my chest over the Army surplus air mattress, pulled on her cotton panties and disappeared into the night without so much as a see-you-later.

Lila had always been like that—one of those intense people who went through the sixties like a wine taster, sampling each vintage and moving on. FSM, SDS, shooting pads in the Haight, the Hell's Angels, bus trips with Kesey's Pranksters, sunshine at the Fillmore, communes in Taos— she did it all. The first time I met her we were being fire-hosed down the steps of San Francisco City Hall at the HUAC protest in May 1960. Even then she was more into it than I, taking a policeman down into the wet cement with her and giving him a quick knee to the groin.

I'm not sure what made Lila that way. Maybe it was her

proper Bostonian background, the old shipping family back on Lewisberg Square. She went around Berkeley like a barefoot Grace Kelly with long blonde hair flowing over her olive sweater and willowy legs stretching through a pair of corduroy hip-huggers. Everyone I knew wanted to nail her, whether he said it or not. But I thought she was something special. And our last night together in 1967 I was hoping for more than a quick fuck before the demonstration.

It didn't happen.

I left the Bay Area a few weeks later and though I thought about her all the time, I can't remember seeing Lila until one quiet evening last May:

I was at home playing solitaire Clue, trying to get a hit on my crusty hash pipe. My token was in the study. I rolled the die and advanced five spaces into the dining room. I sat back to consider the possibilities—Mr. Green had eliminated himself and Professor Plum had a foolproof alibi. He was in the conservatory with Miss Scarlet for the entire afternoon. And doubtless Mr. White would not take his life with his own hands.

So Colonel Mustard or Mrs. Peacock. But which one? Which one?

I drew on the pipe again and rolled the die.

Four.

That would do perfectly, take me right into the hall to break this case wide open. I picked up my token. But just as I began to count off the spaces, I heard a knock on the door. Or thought I did. The stereo was up and I was wearing headphones. But someone was being insistent. The rap of knuckles on frosted glass came piercing right through Stevie Wonder.

I pulled off the phones and checked my watch. It was twenty-eight past eleven, pretty late for visitors. I slipped on some pajama bottoms and walked to the door. Switching on the porch light, I could see the silhouette of a woman against the glass.

"Who is it?" I asked, leaving on the chain.

"A volunteer for Senator Miles Hawthorne. As you may know, Senator Hawthorne is running in the Democratic Presidential Primary next month." The voice was thin, mechanical. I peered out through the crack but the face was shrouded in darkness. "We would like to know where you rate the Senator on a scale of four: 1—favorable . . . 2—somewhat favorable . . . 3—undecided and 4—very unfavorable."

"I'll probably support him." Hawthorne volunteers had been combing our neighborhood for days. I had seen them climbing the hills in their Volkswagens and Datsuns, a lilliputian army of college students and suburban matrons. But they never came at night.

"Would that be one, then?"

"Yeah."

She paused as a motorcycle roared down Echo Park Boulevard.

"We welcome your support for Senator Hawthorne. Every voter in California is important to the campaign. Will you be needing an absentee ballot or transportation to the polls on the day of the primary?"

"Not if I can help it."

I began to close the door but she blocked it with her foot.

"Would you mind answering a few questions for our voter preference survey?"

"At this hour?"

"We're pressed for time, Mr. . . . er . . . Wine. And there are so many voters to cover."

I released the chain to get a better look at her. The light came through from the living room and I could see an attractive leggy young woman with short blonde hair and sharp, almost thrusting green eyes. She was wearing a simple Mexican shift with yellow and blue stitching and a large HAWTHORNE button between her breasts. In her left hand she held a pair of granny glasses and in her right a clipboard with a computer print-out and some campaign literature. The top sheet read "Hawthorne Speaks Out on the Aged."

"The preference survey only takes three to six minutes. May I come in, please?"

I backed up and let her pass. She walked into my living room and sat on the sofa, pausing to stare for a moment at the hash pipe propped against the top of the Clue set. Between the revolver and the rope were two joints of Michoacan grass. Normally I wouldn't leave them out in front of a complete stranger, but Hawthorne was said to favor decriminalization. He was said to favor a lot of things, like guaranteed minimum income and national health insurance. But then he was a Democratic politician at campaign time.

"Have you ever considered working for Senator Hawthorne?" she asked.

"No, not really."

"But you *do* support him."

"I said I did."

I sat down opposite her and waited for the voter preference survey. But it didn't come. She didn't say a word. Instead she put on her granny glasses and examined me at close range, then she turned to take in the rest of the room. The bed was unmade, the dirty dishes stacked in the sink. The stereo was on the floor by the closet with a few records scattered in front. The poster of Lenny Bruce tacked to the bathroom door had a long rip down the center.

"That's all there is," I said. "Outside there's a '47 Buick which some people might call a classic but I swear is a heap."

She didn't smile.

I took a closer look at her. She had freckles on her face and legs and a tiny mole on her left chin. It was then that I recognized Lila.

"Hello, Moses. Do I look very different?"

"Not at all. But you sounded so solemn . . . like a canvasser for the Watchtower or something."

"Sorry about that, but I was told to make certain you supported the Senator before I invited you."

"Invited me to what?"

She didn't answer right away. She stood and walked over toward me, removing her granny glasses. She had changed. The hair was different and her bearing was more mature, more self-assured. In her late twenties she was far prettier than I had remembered her. I wondered what she thought of me.

"Some people at Hawthorne headquarters are waiting to speak with you," she said. "Important people."

"About what?"

She shrugged and looked down at the coffee table, pushing Colonel Mustard three spaces forward with her left hand, up to the entrance of the library.

"Do what they ask you, Moses, for the sake of Senator Hawthorne."

"Senator Hawthorne?"

"Well, then for me. For the old days at Berkeley when we sat all night on the terrace talking about Camus."

She watched my response. For a moment it was as real as the table in front of us—Lila riding through Sather Gate on a Raleigh with a green bookbag over her shoulder; me, standing in the quadrangle watching her with a copy of *Dissent* in my hand, twenty years old.

"I'll try it," I said.

Lila seemed pleased.

2

ALTHOUGH THE LIGHTS were on in the reception room, Hawthorne's headquarters appeared deserted when we arrived twenty minutes later. Lila Shea tapped on the window. I could hear voices and footsteps from a rear corridor. Somebody shouted and then there was a loud thud like a sack of fertilizer landing at the bottom of a chute.

"What was that?" I asked.

She shook her head. A Ford pickup screeched around the block. A dark figure was slumped over in the front seat between two others. Seconds later they had disappeared down Wilshire.

Lila and I exchanged looks. She tapped on the window again. A plump young man in a batik tie poked his head through one of the doors. As soon as he saw who it was, he came out and opened the lock for us. We were introduced and he told me his name was Nate Sugars in a phony basso which indicated he expected me to be impressed. I wasn't at first, then remembered an article in *Newsweek* about an Ivy League computer whiz kid working for Hawthorne's campaign. I took a better look at him. He couldn't have been much more than nineteen. Most of the lard around his middle still looked like baby fat. His shirtsleeves were rolled up and he had a sharp blue pencil behind his ear.

"What was that noise?" Lila asked him.

"Some nut trying to break in. Sebastian took care of him."

Sugars and Lila Shea guided me through the dimly lit corridors past the rows of files and long bank of phones to the rear conference room where the smoke curled up from a tight little circle of cigars. It looked like an old Edward G. Robinson movie.

"Moses Wine." A dark, angular man in his mid-thirties shot his hand out to me. "I'm Sam Sebastian. Senator Hawthorne's L.A. County Coordinator." He wore an expensive voile shirt under a reindeer-patterned sweater vest.

A couple of older pols in shirtsleeves and wide regimental ties turned toward me with bleary-eyed expressions. Sebastian signalled them to leave with Sugars and Lila Shea. The county coordinator then walked around me and shut the door, locking it with a bolt and chain. "Can't be too careful," he explained.

"So I've seen." He seemed confused by my reference. "Those characters peeling out in the Ford pickup," I explained.

"Oh, that. Nothing." He waved his hand in a gesture of dismissal. "We get them all the time. There're a lot of messed-up people in this country. Their parents expect too much of them."

Sebastian motioned for me to sit down. On the blackboard behind him was a minute-by-minute of the Senator's campaign stops for tomorrow. At 10:15 in the morning he would dedicate a swimming pool in Watts.

"Steak kew from Wong's." Sebastian held up a white container. "A little heavy on the cornstarch."

I shook my head and he nodded, taking a seat opposite

me. His eyes were black and motionless. His lips were thin and he had a habit of moistening them every few seconds with the tip of his tongue.

I could see him studying my face. "You don't look like my idea of a private detective," he said. "But then nobody looks like anybody's idea of anything anymore. . . . When do you want to start?"

"Start what?"

"Helping Senator Hawthorne make this country into something worthwhile . . . what we're all here for."

"Oh," I said.

The county coordinator continued to study me openly. "Suspicious of working within the system?" he asked without waiting for a reply. "I was too. Eight, nine months ago I wouldn't have dreamed I'd be working for an establishment politician. Now . . ." He picked up a coffee stirrer for emphasis. "Extreme times demand flexible approaches."

"Get to the point, Sebastian."

"California is the crucial test. The nomination hinges on it. Everybody knows that. Right now it couldn't be closer. Anything we do could turn it around. The slightest rumor, innuendo. We guard against any eventuality, but then this sonofabitch comes along." He threw open his palms like a trial lawyer or a minister who had just revealed some self-evident truth.

"What sonofabitch?" I asked.

"Eppis."

"Eppis?"

"Howard Eppis, chairman of the Free Amerika Party, author of *Rip It Off.*"

Mindless drivel, I thought. "What's wrong with him?"

"He endorsed us."

I started to laugh. The whole thing was very funny. "Come on, Sebastian. I thought you and your senator were great progressives. One lousy radical hops on the band-wagon and it's panic city."

Sebastian wasn't amused. He wrinkled his brow sternly and hitched up his double-knit slacks. "Eppis isn't the only radical who's backed our campaign. A lot of them have. We encourage everyone to work within the system for change ... as long as they stay inside realistic guidelines." Sebastian paused for a moment, then leaned forward as if to share a confidence. "But Eppis is different. We could never contact him. Still can't. He never answers our calls or letters. Finally we tried to visit him in person. No dice. He wasn't in. No one knows where he is. He just seems to have vanished. . . . Then, a couple of days ago, these started arriving at the homes of selected Democratic registrants in the San Gabriel Valley."

He unfolded a manila envelope and passed me a mimeographed sheet. It was an ugly flyer with portraits of Lenin, Mao and Senator Hawthorne across the top and a larger photograph of Howard Eppis in the middle. I read the copy:

Brothers and Sisters—Join me in supporting Senator Miles Hawthorne in his quest for the Presidency. I have talked personally with Senator Hawthorne and am convinced he is a great revolutionary. He will do for Amerika what Mao and Lenin have done for China and Russia. Vote for Hawthorne! Stuff the ballot boxes for him if you can!!!

Howard Eppis' signature was on the bottom above the logo of the Free Amerika Party (FAP). On the opposite side of the page was a photograph of Eppis and Hawthorne shaking hands at some political rally.

"Toilet paper, isn't it?" Sebastian watched my reaction as I held onto the edges of the flyer.

"How many did they send out?"

"A few hundred so far. You can keep this one, if you want."

"What do you want me to do with it?"

"Find out where it came from."

I didn't say anything. The county coordinator tugged at his cuffs to make sure his shirt was straight. I could hear Lila Shea's voice out in the corridor, then the ringing of a telephone. Sebastian leaned in toward me again and gripped on the back of my chair. "I can't understand what Eppis expects to gain by this, or even if he's acting on his own. But whoever's behind it, we've got to stop him and fast."

"Do you have any ideas?" I asked.

Sebastian's answer was interrupted by a knock on the door. "May I come in?" It was Sugars. I couldn't tell how long he had been standing there. The young wizard entered and took a seat to my right, extracting a panatella from his shirt pocket, one of those eighty-five-cent Jamaican jobs with dark wrappers. "Are you going to help us?" he asked me.

"I don't know. Normally I find the Democratic Party about as attractive as a den of vipers. Old guard and re-formers." I watched them. Sugars lit his cigar waiting for me to continue. "But in this case I kind of owe it to a friend of mine in your campaign. I might be persuaded to try it for a few days." Sugars smiled, although neither he nor Sebastian appeared to know who my friend was. "But I do this for a living, of course. I'm not a volunteer for Haw-thorne."

Abruptly the smiles faded. The two men exchanged a look.

"I thought they called you the People's Detective," said Sugars, not without some sarcasm.

"The papers say you guys have a million four in campaign contributions. You're not going to tell me that all came from welfare families."

"Look," said Sebastian, pointing at me with the coffee stirrer. "Our budget's a lot tighter than you think. . . ."

"I come cheap, Sebastian. Three hundred a week plus expenses. Compare that with what you pay your high-priced media men and razzle-dazzle pollsters."

Sugars didn't flinch.

Sebastian turned to him and the whiz kid got up and walked over to a computer against the side wall. He punched a couple of buttons and a series of cards started pouring into the slots like the questions on a television quiz show. I wondered if it was rigged. Sugars took the top card and handed it to the county coordinator.

"All right," he said. "But it goes no farther than this room. If anybody asks, you're a dietary consultant."

Sebastian unlocked the top right drawer of the desk and counted out three hundred dollars and then another two hundred for expenses. In twenties. I took the money and stuffed it in the breast pocket of my work shirt.

"So I find Eppis and make him stop the smear."

They both nodded. I stood to leave.

"What's the last address you have on him?"

"23 Columbia Drive," said Sebastian. "In Venice. But you needn't bother. It's boarded up tight."

Lila was waiting outside in her Volkswagen. On the way back we didn't talk about what went on at the headquarters. She didn't ask me about it and I wasn't sure what she knew. We talked about old times, the friends we'd had and what happened since. Lila was silent about herself. A few words about graduate work in creative writing at San Francisco State and something about going to Europe to find herself, but then nothing. A large gap of nearly half a decade—as if she dissolved in some Parisian cafe then reemerged years later as a campaign worker for Senator Hawthorne. The lapse seemed peculiar to me at the time, but I didn't press her. I assumed she would fill me in at some later date.

We drove up Alvarado and into the Echo Park Hills. Lila's fingers brushed the inside of my leg as she shifted up and down. I watched her, making no attempt to move away. But when she pulled up at my house, she leaned over and opened the door.

"A private dick," she said. "I never would have guessed."

"Neither would I."

3

THE NEXT MORNING I got up with a sharp headache. I didn't think I was going to like this case. Sebastian wasn't so bad. And it was good to see Lila again. But Sugars reminded me of one of those adolescent old men I used to know at law school before I quit, the kind that paraded in three-piece suits discussing torts. Every argument had two sides. Pretending to be fair and pragmatic, they debated everything to death so they would never have to be responsible for a decision. In twenty years they'd be just like my New York relatives, riding through Harlem in their late-model Lincoln limousines with the windows rolled up for the air-conditioning and the radio tuned to WBAI.

Besides, I didn't have any particular bone to pick with Howard Eppis. He was only a second-rate radical, doing his bit. If he wanted to spoil Hawthorne's chances, that was his privilege.

I rolled over and reached for the hash pipe on the headboard. Maybe a few good hits would clear my temples. But the last of the hash had turned to ashes. I got up and looked at myself in the mirror. My eyes were bloodshot and my hair was getting pretty stringy. I was in bad need of a shampoo. I bent down and threw some water on my face. Then I went over to the stove and started to make some instant coffee. I wondered if the Buick was going to make it up the hill this morning.

Thirty minutes later I was wending my way through the back streets of Venice past those faded Victorian mansions which were once the elegant beach homes of the rich, looking for 23 Columbia Drive. I found it at the end of a cul-de-sac, a peculiar old duck complete with a widow's walk and a pair of wooden lions guarding the front door. It was boarded up all right, with grass high enough to thresh and dandelions crawling through the door jams. A dusty For Sale sign from Pacific Properties, Marina del Rey, stood by the driveway. The front door was locked, but around the side I found a crack in one of the window shutters and looked in. The place was a morgue. Soot covered everything and the bathtub was coated with grime. The ceiling was stained an ugly mildew brown, and the cobwebs between the light fixtures were thick enough to swing on. If anybody had been living here in the last year, he was probably in a hospital by now sweating out some rare tropical disease. I backed away from the window and looked down the other side. Someone was watching me from the neighboring house through the slits of a Venetian blind.

I returned to my car and drove off, heading toward the ocean. The decaying monuments of another age soon disappeared, giving way to the pre-fab mausoleums of our own—low-slung motel structures with names like Neptune's Kingdom and Tahitian Singles Village West. The Marina itself was set up like a second-rate Disneyland. Pacific Properties stood behind a macramé fishnet between Sid's Surf-o-rama and the Mermaid's Booknook. A plastic parrot over the door croaked, "Ahoy, shipmates! Beach house or permanent home. . . . Buy Pacific!"

I entered and was greeted by a handsome, greying man

in yachting attire who bounded out of a deck chair in the front.

"Good morning. My name is Charlie Flint. May I help you?"

"Yes. I was interested in purchasing real estate in the Venice area."

"And what is your name, sir?"

"Moses Wine."

Flint paused to write my name on a yellow legal pad, then turned up toward me again with the sincere smile of a mortician.

"Well, Mose, you stopped at the right place. Were you thinking beach house, investment property or permanent home?"

"I was thinking permanent home."

"Very good. I'm sure you'll enjoy the relaxed beach life-style. What kind of house were you thinking, Mose, and what kind of figures . . . if you don't mind my asking."

"About four bedrooms at twenty-five thousand dollars."

"Twenty-five thousand."

Flint's smile faded into a pout and then to a kind of awkward smirk. He walked around the side of his desk to a cork bulletin board and skimmed down the list of properties which were arranged by size and location. From behind I could see he was wearing a pair of those Swedish clogs and a rope belt tied in a cinch, pirate style.

"I'm sorry, Mose, but I don't think we have anything in your category at this time. You know it's very difficult to find anything under fifty thousand within a half-mile of the Marina. . . . Will keep an eye out for you though." He turned and extended a limp hand. "Glad you stopped at Pacific."

"Sure you don't have anything, Mr. Flint?"

"I just said . . ."

"What about the place on 23 Columbia Drive?"

For a moment the realtor hesitated, then his hand went

to his forehead as if trying to recall the address. "23 Columbia Drive, let me check our files." He unlocked his bottom drawer and made a show of looking through a cardfile in a metal container, pulling out another card with a photograph and reading from it. From where I was standing, the house didn't look anything like the one on Columbia Drive. "Sorry again, Mose. The owner will only accept an offer over fifty-six thousand dollars. Now if we're talking those kinds of figures..."

"Fifty-six thousand? For that dump?"

"Well...."

"It would take ten grand to fix the plumbing alone."

"We must respect our client's wishes, Mose."

"Who owns the place?"

Flint looked down at the card again, shaking his head and making a supercilious clucking noise.

"What can I say, Mose? Our client has requested that he remain anonymous."

"Let me see that!"

I reached forward and yanked the card out of his hand. Flint lunged at me, but I stepped away from him to the other side of the desk.

"Give that back, Mr. Wine!"

I looked at the card. It contained the specifications for an expensive beach front property at the tip of the Marina, a Spanish villa selling for $119,000.

"All right, Flint, what's the deal?"

"What deal?"

"How come you're not telling me who owns that property?"

"It's just as I said. Our client prefers to remain anonymous. You were getting edgy so I thought the simplest way would...." He was becoming conciliatory again. "Look, Mose, I don't see why you care so much about that house. It's not even a good buy at twenty-five thousand. I wouldn't recommend it to my worst enemy."

"Come off it, Flint. All I have to do is take the street address to the city engineer's office for a legal description of the property and then go down to Title Insurance for the name of the owner."

"I wouldn't waste your time, Mr. Wine. It's registered under an alias. And now, if you'll excuse me, I have some important calls to make."

He walked off to one of the desks in the rear and sat down, dialing a number rapidly while keeping his eyes glued on me. I couldn't figure out why they left a For Sale sign on the property unless there was some real intention of selling it. Possibly it was an oversight. Or possibly it was a way to find out who was snooping around the premises. I tried to listen to what Flint said, but he was speaking very softly. He had curled his fingers over his mouth so his lips couldn't be read. I started out. A mother and daughter entered the agency as I reached the door. Flint gave them the peace sign.

On my way to the car, I stopped at the Mermaid's Booknook and bought a copy of *Rip It Off*. An impressive stack was piled up beside the checkout counter next to a poster of Eppis' grinning Harpo Marx face. With all those royalties, his publishers must have had some way of getting ahold of him—if they would tell me. I tossed the book into the back seat of the car and drove off. Pulling onto Lincoln Boulevard, I turned on the radio. I heard chimes and a cutesy little theme song played on the ocarina. It was one of those luncheon talk shows filled with mindless chatter against a background of tinkling glasses. The host had a voice like salt-water taffy on a desert rock.

"Hello, again, friends. We've a surprise for you this afternoon, our town's most famous political couple. Is it true you two powerbroking Wilsons are working full time behind the scenes on the Dillworthy campaign?"

"Yes, it is, Bill. Arthur Dillworthy's our man."

"What stratagems are you planning to bolster your candidate and derail Senator Hawthorne in his quest for the nomination?"

"I don't think that's a problem, Bill. Arthur Dillworthy's record speaks for itself. And I can promise you, one week before the date of the primary the people of this state will know where Miles Hawthorne stands too. They'll see he's too far out of the mainstream of American life."

I turned to a Spanish language station.

In my rearview mirror I could see two large men in pastel banlon shirts seated in the front of a green Chevelle with an out-of-state license. One of them held what looked like a miniature camera in his right hand and appeared to be photographing my car. Trying to get a better look, I slowed down at the entrance to a shopping mall to let them come up alongside, but they turned off into the parking lot and vanished at the other end behind a bank.

Farther along Lincoln, I stopped at a local bar to make a quick call to the Scotsford Press, Eppis' publishers. A group of Chicano businessmen were seated at a corner table drinking Tecate from the can. I walked around them to the phone which was attached to the wall beside the jukebox. As I dialed, a Mexican woman wearing a dress like Lila Shea's sat down at the table nearest me. She had one of those exquisite Indian faces like the peasant women in Orozco murals, but made up with a misty-green mascara around the eyes. I was staring at her feeling a little weak-kneed when I connected with the Scotsford receptionist in New York.

"273-4907."

"I'd like to speak with Howard Eppis' editor."

"One mo-ment."

The Chicana ordered vermouth and lit a cigarette, blowing the smoke in a steady stream toward me. She wore the sharp, flowery perfume that Latin women seem to prefer and a gold pendant in the shape of an Aztec god around her neck.

"Lucy Garber's office."

"I'd like to speak with Lucy Garber. This is Moses Wine calling."

"Does Ms. Garber know you?"

"No, I . . ."

"Ms. Garber is very busy."

"I'm a private detective. I'd like to speak with her about one of her authors."

"We have a policy not to discuss our authors, sir."

"You'd better make an exception."

"I see. . . . One second."

The secretary put the telephone on hold. The Chicana stood up and walked in my direction. I could hear the nylon rubbing between her legs. She smiled at me, leaning up against the jukebox. I reached over and handed her a dime for the machine. She dropped the coin in the slot and pushed two buttons. A jazz samba by João Gilberto. She started swaying to the music.

"What's your name?" I asked her.

"Alora," she said.

I was about to say something else when I was interrupted by a voice on the line.

"Lucy Garber speaking. Who's calling?"

"Hello, Ms. Garber. My name is Moses Wine."

"You're a private detective, Mr. Wine?"

"Yes, I'm working for a client who must get in contact with one of your authors . . . Howard Eppis."

"I don't disclose information about my authors."

"I know, but this is very important to my client, Ms. Garber. It could be life or death."

"Who is your client, Mr. Wine?"

I watched Alora sway back and forth to the samba. Her

hips moved in an undulating motion. The inside of her thighs was the color of café au lait on a summer morning. Her dress wasn't like Lila Shea's. It was much tighter and shorter.

"Mr. Wine? Are you still there?"

"Yes, I'm here."

"I need to know who your client is before I can say anything."

"Look, Ms. Garber, I can assure you all we want is an address . . . some way of locating him."

The record ended and Alora smiled at me again. I smiled back.

"Just some way of locating him, Ms. Garber. This may sound crazy, but the political future of our country could be in the balance."

It sounded crazy to me. Alora finished extinguishing her cigarette in an ashtray on top of the jukebox. "Another drink?" I asked, but she shook her head. Then she waved goodbye to me with the tips of her fingers, turned and walked away, heading around the corner into the front room. Too bad.

"If that's what you want, Mr. Wine, you've called the wrong place."

"You send him royalty checks, don't you? He must be making a million."

"Not quite that much, Mr. Wine. Now if you'll . . ."

"All right, Ms. Garber, I'm working for the Hawthorne campaign."

A moment's silence. "Senator Miles Hawthorne?"

"Correct."

"I see." She sounded impressed.

"Where can I find Howard Eppis?"

"I wish I knew. I haven't seen the bastard since he wrote *Rip It Off* here in my office in three days flat two years ago."

"What about a mailing address?"

"He changed it six months ago to a post box in Los Angeles. But I haven't had any personal correspondence from him either. He never writes back. If you knew the crap I had to go through to get him published in the first place. . . . Hey, what's going on? I kind of like Senator Hawthorne. I mean, he's a politician and all, but it might even be worth registering this time. You know what I mean?"

"Yeah. What post office box, Ms. Garber?"

"Post office box? Did I say that? I meant General Delivery. General Delivery, Los Angeles, California. And, hey, if you do find Howard, tell him I want to talk with him. I've got a dynamite idea for a new book he could really get into—communes in Central Africa. We might even be able to arrange travel expenses."

"Is that all, Ms. Garber?"

"Yeah, but please don't tell anyone I told you that much. They'd use any excuse to get rid of me at this place."

She hung up. Some lot she told me. General Delivery, Los Angeles. That was about as useful as the 1942 Yellow Pages. The operator called back with the overtime charges. I told her to bill them to Sam Sebastian at Hawthorne Headquarters and clicked off.

The businessmen were on their second beers as I walked around them toward the front. The jukebox had segued into a nauseating Jacques Brel ballad. The air-conditioning wasn't working and I wasn't feeling good. But when I reached the door, a lovely brown leg stretched out blocking my path. It was Alora, seated at the last table in the room nursing the end of her vermouth. She gazed at me with her inscrutable Indian eyes, black as an Aztec night. A moon goddess at a jungle sacrifice.

"Hello."

"Where are we going?"

"I'm waiting for my sister."

"Can't you leave her a note?"

I reached into my pocket and handed her a pencil. She looked at me for a moment, then bent over a cocktail napkin and wrote: "Dear Sister: I had to leave early. See you tonight." She handed the note to the bartender.

"It's for my sister," she said.

The bartender's lips curled almost imperceptibly and he folded the napkin in half, placing it under a bottle of maraschino cherries.

Alora took me by the hand. I pushed open the swinging doors and we walked into the glaring sunlight.

"How about my place?" she said. "My car." She pointed to a battered Studebaker at the end of an alley. "It's not far."

We headed down the alley. Alora stood close to me. I could feel her warm thigh, her naked brown arm.

Halfway down, I shoved her into a doorway.

"Hey! What're you doing?"

I kicked open the service door and, grabbing her by the wrist, pulled her down a corridor. I pinned her up against the concrete wall next to a wire window.

"Okay, *hermana*, who're you working for? Who put you up to this?"

"I don't know what you're talking about."

"You don't?!" I turned her around to the window, holding onto her arm. Outside, parked directly in front of her Studebaker, was the green Chevy. The two big men in banlon shirts sat in the front seat watching the building apprehensively. I could read the license plate: 328KLR, Nevada.

"Who are they?" I said, twisting her arm hard behind her back until I could hear her groan.

"I don't know . . . goddamnit!"

"Do you expect me to believe that?" I twisted a little harder. I would have broken her arm right off if she hadn't been a woman. Those bastards outside would have taken me for a ride and dropped me under the nearest railroad bridge for sure.

"I don't know who they are. I swear. They just..." At that moment, one of the men noticed us in the window. He punched his partner, who floored the Chevy in reverse and gunned out of there, leaving tracks halfway across Lincoln Boulevard. "They...they...gave me a hundred dollars if I'd lead you out here. I work over at the Venus Massage... in Panorama City."

I reached into her pocketbook and found two crisp new U.S. Grants. She was trembling all over. Maybe she was worried I would take her money. I stuffed them back in the bag and walked out in the sun.

4

SOMEBODY HAD DONE his homework. There was no Venus Massage in Panorama City and license plate 328KLR, Nevada, was privately listed.

I lay on my bed under the Tensor light reading *Rip It Off*, Chapter Three, "Crash Pads." It was a dreary production filled with the cliches of the late and middle sixties set in an archaic psychedelic type. His prose sounded like a bad underground disc jockey on uppers. I wondered who would pay $2.95 for the privilege of hearing about this or that "trip" or of discovering what was "groovy" and "right on." Some acid-damaged fifteen-year-old from Des Moines, maybe, or a frustrated housewife in Waco, Texas, hoping for a way out into the cool world. I had bought it, of course, but I was looking for clues, some indication where Eppis might be hiding, betrayed by his own hand. Unfortunately, of the crash pads listed, only one happened to be in Southern California and that was the L.A. County Beach, a hiding place some thirty miles in length and a little too open to hold a mimeograph machine. I had turned to the chapter on "Free Food" when I remembered I knew a friend of Eppis'— or at least an acquaintance—Earl Speidel, the record pro-

ducer. Three or four years back, right after the Chicago Convention and at the height of Howard's celebrity, Earl had
cut an album with him and other radicals called *Voices of
Dissent.* Not long ago, I had seen it remaindered at Thriftymart for seventy-nine cents next to *Gerry and the Pace-
makers Gear the Merseyside Beat.*

I reached for the phone to call Earl, but before I could
dial information for the number of Grit Records, I was interrupted by another voice on the line. It was someone
working for Sebastian. The county coordinator wanted to
see me right away.

Finding a parking space in front of Hawthorne Headquarters was nearly impossible. There were still two weeks
before the primary, but the surrounding blocks of Wilshire
were bumper to bumper. In front of the office itself, the
activity was fierce. High-spirited college boys ran up and
down the stairs carrying large cartons of campaign literature
to a pair of Dodge vans blocking traffic in the middle of the
boulevard. A crew from Abbey Rents were setting up a scaf-
fold along the sidewalk. Voter registrars strode up the street
with their large grey ledgers and stacks of petitions. I rode
up the elevator to the main lobby. The room was jammed
with volunteers making phone calls, typing addresses and
yakking furiously to each other. I walked up to the receptionist, a harried young lad in a USC sweatshirt.

"I'd like to see Sam Sebastian. I'm Moses Wine."

"What's this about?" The receptionist gave me a long
skeptical look indicating I'd better have some high-powered
explanation to get to see a heavy like Sebastian.

"I'm the dietary consultant."

"The dietary consultant," he nodded with a shit-eating
grin on his face. "Sorry, my man, but Sam's in conference.
High priority stuff. If you'd like to leave a message?"

I wanted to push his face in the IBM typewriter but we
were blinded as a movie crew switched on the arc lights to

film Conrad Kimble, the daytime TV star, licking envelopes for Senator Hawthorne. A make-up man rushed forward with a hairbrush.

"This isn't a good time, my man," explained Mr. USC. "They're caucussing in Colorado."

"I don't give a shit if they're caucussing in the Caucasus. Sebastian just called me. I'm supposed to see him.

"Look." I reached for my wallet. "This ten spot says you buzz Sebastian on your intercom and tell him the dietary consultant is here and I'll be in there in ten seconds."

"Okay," said USC. "But you lose and you give it to the campaign."

Magnanimous bastard.

He rang Sebastian's office.

"There's a guy here who says he's the dietary consultant."

"What are you waiting for? Send him in."

I stared the receptionist right in the eye. He wasn't moving. At length he opened the top drawer and pulled out a ten-dollar bill. I took it and folded it in my pocket.

"Aren't you going to donate it to the campaign?"

"No."

When I entered Sebastian's office, most of the lights were out and the county coordinator was slumped over the table. He had rings around his eyes as big as Pismo clams and the shocked expression of a man who has just been punched in the stomach. Sugars was in the corner hugging his slide rule like a security blanket. Two telephone lines were flashing on the desk, but neither of them was answering. I couldn't figure what all the depression was about. The Harris Poll that morning had shown Hawthorne edging ahead of Dillworthy for the first time, thirty-seven to thirty-six with fourteen percent for the other candidates and thirteen percent undecided. They couldn't be that scared of the undecided vote. It had usually gone in their favor. And with all the guilt-stricken celebrities contributing to their war chest, I would have guessed they had it in the bag.

Sebastian didn't say anything but twisted painfully in his chair and pushed a photograph over to me. I picked it up and examined it carefully. It was a police glossy of a dismembered body. The legs were squashed into bloody stubs and the right arm was missing. One of the shoulders had been crushed and the head turned around in the opposite direction. The top of the cranium had been pierced and the brains were spilling out to the side. The torso itself had been so disfigured you could barely make out it was the corpse of a woman. I felt sick to my stomach. Sebastian pushed over another photograph. It showed a half-demolished Volkswagen upended at the side of a cliff. The concave roof rested on a concrete slab just above where the driver would have sat.

"Lila Shea," I mumbled, barely audible.

Sebastian nodded.

"When did it happen?"

"Thirty minutes after you left here. Off a cliff below Cerro Gordo."

"Sons of bitches."

The campaign manager reached for a paper cup and crumpled it. Outside I could hear the television director yelling to Conrad Kimble. The cameraman hadn't been ready when the star glued the address sticker on the envelope. Could he try it once more? Sugars joined us at the table, placing his slide rule in a leather sleeve. The photographs of Lila Shea lay between us. I concentrated instead on the benign visage of Miles Hawthorne tacked to the far wall.

"What about the police?" I asked.

"They're investigating. A half-empty bottle of barbiturates was found in her glove compartment."

He hesitated.

"What else?"

"Nothing much. Everything else was destroyed in the crash, except for two cartons of Hawthorne literature and the computer print-outs in the trunk."

"Shit," said Sugars, banging his fist as if the presence of the campaign literature were the unkindest cut of all. "It's murder, isn't it?"

"Probably."

"Who did it?"

I shrugged. I wasn't about to tell him about Nevada license plate 328KLR or my run-in with Alora. Or, for that matter, about the excessive price asked for the decrepit mansion on Columbia. Not now, anyway. Sugars pulled out another cigar from his vest pocket and lit it. It looked pretentious against his premature corpulence.

"You'd better find out soon," he said, pointing the cigar. "This thing could blow up into a disaster for us."

"Yeah."

"Those bastards are out to stop us any way they can."

"Yeah." I watched Sugars smoke, detesting him for caring more about his candidate than the slaughtered woman. Sebastian noticed this and turned to the younger man with a discouraging look.

"Why was Lila Shea chosen to come to my house?" I asked. "You could have sent anyone . . . or telephoned."

"She wasn't chosen," said Sebastian. "She came to me." I waited for him to continue. "She was the one who brought me the Eppis flyer."

"Did you verify it?"

"Of course we did." He flared momentarily. "The flyers were mailed. Another batch turned up in Santa Monica this morning."

"Who suggested you hire a private detective?"

The two men looked at each other.

"She did . . . and she suggested I hire you."

"And then I checked you out," Sugars chimed in. "Thoroughly."

"Why didn't you tell me this before?"

"It didn't seem important."

"Oh." I picked up a pamphlet from the table: "Democratic Candidates for Delegates to Party National Convention—Certified List." I thumbed through it. Each candidate had 238 delegates and 103 alternates pledged to him. They were listed with their cities of origin. I recognized the names of a few entertainers and some secondline politicians.

"May I keep this?"

"Sure," said Sebastian.

I stood to leave, sliding the pamphlet into the hip pocket of my jeans, and opened the door without looking back at them.

"Don't give me excuses," one young organizer shouted into his phone as I crossed through the front room. "We need that precinct and we need it bad. Get it canvassed." Then he hung up.

5

THE NEXT MORNING a dense fog had blown in all the way from the ocean to Echo Park, about eighteen miles. When I went outside, the windshield of the Buick was covered with moisture. I wiped it off with a chamois cloth and let the engine run for a while. The tail pipe belched like an old man with catarrh. The parking lights weren't working and the carburetor made a peculiar pinging noise. I checked the tires all around. They were as bald as a Mexican hairless. I should have done something about this, taken the heap into a garage or into Glendale for a new set of tires, but I got in and drove toward the Hollywood Freeway instead. It was Saturday. My day for the kids.

The fog was burning off as I headed through Cahuenga Pass in the Valley and transferred to the Ventura Freeway. Out in the distance a fierce smog was building up at the base of the San Gabriels. The sky was beginning to look like steamed piss. I turned off the freeway at Laurel Canyon Boulevard and made a left up the hill into the canyon. Soon the Valley tract homes faded from view and I climbed higher into the Santa Monica Mountains, the dense foliage folding about me. Taking one of the twisting side streets off Mulholland, I wound my way up to Suzanne's house and parked beneath the jacaranda tree. Her guru Madas was squatting on the front porch in a meditation position, middle-aged muscles rippling on his bare chest. His trance must not have been very deep, because I could see him follow me with his eyes as I tramped past him and around the house.

Jacob was in the backyard watering the flowers and shaking his sheep dog hair like Ringo Starr. Simon, his one-year-old brother, watched in admiration from the playpen. They both wore yellow tee-shirts and Suzanne had sewn zodiac patches on the seats of their pants. Simon was a Gemini and Jacob a Scorpio like me.

I stood there for a moment, realizing how glad I was to see them. Then I sneaked up quietly, picking up Simon first, hugging him to me and feeling his tiny ribs like chicken bones against my side. Next Jacob jumped into my arms, nuzzling my neck and smearing peanut butter on my shirt collar. They felt good. I could see Suzanne through the window. She was making a carrot cake and smiling to herself.

"Mommy needs money," said Jacob.

"What for?"

"The gas."

"Twenty-four dollars," Suzanne called through the window.

"I thought I paid for that," I said, moving toward her.

"You owed three months." She came out the back door with Jacob's sandals and an extra pair of diapers for Simon.

"I don't have it. All I've got is enough for the kids' lunches. Why don't you get him to pay for it? He lives here." I nodded toward Madas.

"That's your responsibility. Besides, next week Madas is taking me to Squaw Valley to meet Swami Sri Prasnamurti. They're having a meeting of the Human Potential Movement."

"Great."

"Well, have a good time." She handed me the sandals and Simon's diapers.

I turned and carried the boys around the front past where Madas was sitting in the lotus position with the tips of his fingers over his eyelids, the picture of inscrutability.

"Reached the astral plane?" I asked him, dumping the kids in the back seat of my car. He didn't say anything. I pulled out slowly, careful not to dent the fender of the guru's powder blue XKE. In the rearview mirror I could see his holiness watching me like a hawk.

"I want three roast beef sandwiches and four macaroons," said Jacob, bouncing on the seat as we coasted down Laurel Canyon Boulevard to Hollywood, then right on Fairfax. The streets were crowded with Orthodox Jews in payas and Miami Beach matrons in spangled pumps walking with their hippie sons.

"How come four macaroons?" I asked.

"Four 'cause I'm four." The logic was indisputable.

We parked in front of Handleman's Bookstore. Jacob peered in the window at the display of books and ancient manuscripts: The Talmud, the Midrash, the new translation of Rosenzweig's *Star of Redemption*. Old man Handleman waved to us and I picked up Simon so he could see him. Then we moved on down the street past Kugelman's Bakery and Wholesale Candystore to Canter's. I took a ticket at the delicatessen counter while Jacob pushed his face up against the glass in front of the dill pickles and stuffed derma.

"Let's get something for Aunt Sonya," he said.

We bought three roast beef sandwiches, two pastramis, pickles, potato salad, some macaroons, three bottles of Dr. Brown's cream soda and halvah. Then we left the store and crossed the street to the Fairfax Senior Citizens Center.

The main lounge smelled of Lysol. We pushed through

the revolving door, making our way through the Saturday morning crowd of relatives. On the moveable stage an ancient gentleman in a velvet yamulka sang "Oif'n Pripitchik" in front of a Yiddish dance band. Tears were streaming down his face, but the lines of backgammon players at the banquet tables didn't seem to notice. We found Sonya in her purple babushka seated in her usual spot at a rear table opposite her old friend Mr. Bittleman. They were engaged in an argument.

"Mr. Seymour Bittleman—you should pardon the expression—has made a ridiculous misinterpretation of history," she told the boys as they climbed onto her lap. "After seventy years of struggle, he now announces that Kautsky was correct at the Second International ... *Vey es Mir!* ... Don't you remember what Trotsky wrote in 'A letter to Party Meetings,' that the Kautskian line leads to nothing but revisionism and Social Democracy?!"

"The rabbi of Kotzk said: Everything in the world can be imitated except truth. For truth that is imitated is no longer truth." Bittleman grinned and stabbed a piece of codfish with his fork.

"Now what the hell does that mean?" She tugged at her babushka and made a face somewhere between Ethel Merman and La Pasionaria.

"The rabbi of Ger said: I often hear men say they want to throw up the world. But I ask you, is the world yours to throw up?"

"Shut up, Bittleman. I don't want you polluting these children's minds with your cheap religious talk. Next thing you know you'll be putting on a prayer shawl and quoting Hillel."

She turned away from him with a wave and I opened the lunch in front of us. Bittleman snickered and tucked a tiny napkin into his white shirt which was already stained with fish oil.

"We've got a pastrami sandwich for you, Aunt Sonya," said Jacob.

"Good boy," she said, taking the sandwich from him, but her voice was still fuming. "So what's news?" she said, turning to me.

I recounted how I was doing some investigating for Senator Hawthorne's campaign.

"That's news?" she said, sneering at me in disgust and biting off a large hunk of pickle. "Better you should tell me your youngest son is having a lobotomy."

"Come on, Sonya. A man's gotta make a living."

"Some living!" She spread mustard on the pastrami and gobbled it down in three mouthfuls. "I've seen those *chozzers*. Kissing the *tuchases* of old people. Hawthorne? A nothing reformer. A Menshevik. And Dillworthy? Comes around last week grinning like an imbecile. Asks me how I like living at the Center."

"What'd you tell him?"

"The truth—it's a shit-hole!" A younger man in bellbottoms and an obvious wig walked on stage to congratulate the musicians as the band went into "Bei Mir Bist Du Schoen." Sonya looked up at him with obvious disdain and reached for the potato salad. "So the *chozzer* has the nerve to ask me why—what's so bad about it? So I tell him. They treat old people like children and the whole place just exists to make a quick profit. So he says, my dear lady, we'll have to do something about that. And I say, my ass you will; one of your biggest backers owns the place."

At the other end, Bittleman started to laugh in spite of himself, dipping the bottom of his tie in the fish oil.

"What'd he say to that?"

But I didn't wait for an answer. Something had attracted my attention through the front window. A battered Studebaker was parked in front of the Senior Citizens Center. Standing up slowly, I sauntered off toward the men's room and pushed open the door. An oldster was standing at the urinal trying to tinkle. I walked past him and climbed up on the radiator. He looked at me in terror and was about to scream when I smiled at him and put a finger to my lips. Then I turned and, pulling open the window, slipped out onto Beverly Boulevard. I was in the parking lot of a Pup 'n Taco. I crossed the lot to the sidewalk on Fairfax Avenue. Moving up among the shoppers, I came on the Studebaker from behind. Alora wasn't there this time; a Mexican-American man in a fatigue jacket occupied the front seat. He had a pair of binoculars around his neck and was staring directly at the Senior Citizens Center. His expression was so intense it was easy to sneak up on him. I walked up to the Studebaker, opened the door and sat down beside him.

"Looking for somebody?" Before he could answer, I removed his keys from the ignition. "You guys don't give up, do you? Maybe I should just give you a copy of my itinerary. It would save you a lot of effort."

The Chicano turned and gave me a cold stare. "Are you going to get out of my car or am I going to have to call the police?"

"Call the police," I said.

I reached up to the sun visor and pulled out the automobile registration. The car was registered in the name of Alora Vazquez, 3201 $1/4$ Evergreen Way, East Los Angeles. He grabbed the card back and stuffed it in his shirt.

"You shouldn't keep those things in the open if you're going to do this kind of work," I said.

"Get out of here."

"Not very professional. . . . Who're you working for?"

"I'm not working for anybody."

"What about your Vegas buddies?"

"I said I'm not working for anybody. Now get out."

I didn't move.

He stuck his hand inside his fatigue jacket and pulled

out a knife. The leather handle was worn but the blade was sharp enough to cut diamonds.

"I get the message." I twisted the handle but stopped myself when the door was half-open. "Say, you look a little like Alora Vazquez . . . a brother or something."

He flicked the blade against the side of my jeans, carving a neat half-moon in the denim. I nodded to him and got out of the car.

"If it'll save you trouble," I told him, "my next stop is the Grit Recording Studio in Westwood. You can park across the street, but don't try to go inside. They don't allow wetbacks in nice places like that."

I tossed the keys on the seat and headed for the Center.

Back inside, Sonya had resumed her argument with Bittleman. Simon was smearing the potato salad across her plate into a dog-eared copy of Velikovsky's *Worlds in Collision.*

"Ouspensky-Shmoospensky," she was saying. "I don't give a crap for your addle-brained metaphysics. Need I recall at this late date what Bakunin said concerning the ignorance of theological conceptions?"

"What's theorojiggle conlepshuns?" asked Jacob.

"Something for nudniks," said Sonya, patting him on the head as I moved Simon out of reach of the potato salad.

"I'll be back for the kids in a few hours," I said, turning toward the door. "And remember what Marx said of Feuerbach in the *Critique of Hegelian Philosophy.*"

"What was that?"

"Philosophy is nothing but religion rendered into thought hence equally condemnable as just another estrangement from the true essence of man."

"That's right!" said Sonya.

6

H OWARD EPPIS." EARL Speidel mumbled the words with
his feet up on the 12-track board and a reel of white
leader in his mouth. "You always come to me with
the dillies."

"Who else knows all the superstars, Earl?"

The band was warming up and I couldn't quite hear his
reply. It sounded like "Get fucked!" Beneath the giant Altec
A-7's, R. T. Higgins, king of the Texas blues, tuned his guitar
opposite a horn section of white longhairs. The lead trum-
peter leaned against the wall snorting coke from a double-
nostrilled onyx plate.

"Who wants him?" asked Earl, stepping away from the
board to the Dolby. "The FBI or his mother?"

I raised my hand in protest.

"Oh, I forgot. Psychiatrists and private detectives, they
only talk about their clients at cocktail parties."

"When'd you last see him, Earl?"

"Three years ago. When we made the record. What a
depressed sonofabitch."

"Depressed?"

"You're telling me. Eppis was one of those radicals who

37

thought the revolution would be fought and won by March 1, 1969. When his timetable fell through, he went bananas. No wonder she left him."

"Who?"

"What's her name? Great girl. Real smart. Knew the whole Charlie Parker solo on 'Confirmation.' She walked out on him over that madman Procari. Can you blame her?"

Earl signalled to the engineer who flicked the switch. "We're rolling!" The band launched into a blues in the El-more James style, R. T. Higgins out front, wailing with a bottle of Kentucky bourbon propped against the amplifier. A half-dozen hangers-on in the control room kept time smoking joints and munching fortune cookies. I picked one up. It read: "Help Help! I am being held captive by Grit Records!"

When the song was over, Earl congratulated the musicians and told them the day's session was completed. I waited until they had gone.

"Who was she, Earl?"

"I forgot . . . I forgot . . . I'm terrible about names. I flew all the way to London to record the lead singer of the Pink Floyd and I couldn't even remember what to call him."

"What about this Procari?"

"The rich boy who owns this studio . . . or did, until his old man took it away from him. Oscar Procari, Jr., ne'er-do-well son of the financier Oscar Procari, Sr. Flunked out of every school in the East and bankrupted five businesses until he landed here. I would have felt sorry for him if he hadn't been such a pretentious pain in the ass, always whining about his father."

The engineer locked the day's tapes in a metal cabinet and said goodnight. I fingered the last of my roach and walked over to Earl.

"What did Eppis have to do with this?"

"Watch," said Earl, crossing the studio floor past the

door to the echo chamber and a room filled with automated mixing equipment to a wide wall mirror with an Art Deco decal. He pushed the side and the mirror swung open, revealing a hidden passageway. "When Procari first came out here, he wanted to be a record producer, but he didn't know middle C from the man in the moon. So to stay on the good side of the musicians he started staging orgies, providing lots of dope." Earl entered the passageway and I followed him. It was dark and I couldn't make out much from the light in the recording studio. "The orgies escalated. One thing led to another. Procari would do anything kinky for attention."

We came to a small room and Earl switched on a wall lamp. It illuminated a shrine of the most eclectic sort. Paintings of Christ, Merlin, Buddha, Confucius and Satan hung over an altar beneath a gruesome pair of spiked medieval handcuffs and a mace. A tryptich in the tradition of Hieronymous Bosch decorated the far wall beside a chalice and some dried dandelions. The floor was covered with straw mats painted black and purple with a bloody hand outlined in the center.

"The Church of the Five Deities. Procari invented it, based on his own version of the Hell Fire Club and some San Francisco devil cults. He was very successful for a while. He had one of those weird magnetic personalities that could dupe people into believing anything."

"Even Eppis?"

"I don't know. We were into some pretty heavy recording then. Militant political raps. Blacks. Brown power people. Vietnamese. Eppis was out of his league. Depressed. He'd duck back here whenever he got the chance."

"Did you ever see Eppis again . . . after the recording?" We headed back out into the studio.

"Nah. Never heard from him. And he never had to come around for royalties. Those political records never sold shit."

"What happened to Procari?"

"Excommunication from his own church. Procari, Sr., found out about it and was pretty disgusted. I guess he was afraid of the kind of scandal that would ruin his own business. So he cut his son off . . . disowned him totally and sold the building to a Midwestern conglomerate without so much as a phone call. One evening in the middle of a whip ceremony some lawyers arrived with an eviction notice. Procari, Jr., was humiliated. Broke down in front of everyone."

"What'd he do after that?"

"He killed himself. They found his Maserati floating in the ocean off Palos Verdes Peninsula two years ago this spring. He must have driven off the cliff."

"So much for Oscar Procari, Jr."

"Yeah . . . Although a few of his acolytes seem to think he's still alive. But then this city's filled with demented maniacs."

He stopped at the end of the corridor and looked at me. We stood there silent for a moment. Then a thought crossed my mind that I didn't like at all because it gave me the same sinking feeling I had felt the previous day.

"Eppis' girl friend," I said. "Was she a blonde?"

"Yeah."

"With a mole on her left chin?"

"Uhuh."

"Lila."

"That's the one. You know her!" He sounded excited. "She can tell you where Eppis is."

"She's dead."

The smile faded from Earl's lips. He stared at the floor.

"A brilliant girl," he said. "What a goddamn shame. She knew all of Charlie Parker by heart. 'Confirmation,' 'Groovin' High,' 'A Night in Tunisia.' The works."

"I know."

Earl pushed the top of the mirror and we re-entered the

studio. All the lights were out except for a couple of pilots beneath the tape decks and the red exit sign. Through a window of the sound stage, it looked like the engine room of a spaceship or the front end of a great international jet-liner. Mission control, Houston. Thirty-six hours and eleven minutes to blastoff. Earl pulled an impressive ring of keys out of a drawer and let me out of the building. The midday smog had turned vermilion. It was already twilight.

7

THAT EVENING I watched the first televised debate between Dillworthy and Hawthorne while my sons tried to wreck my Clue set with a plastic letter opener. I took that away quickly, but while my back was turned Simon spilled half the contents of a Gerber's jar into the game tokens. That's the younger generation for you. No respect for Colonel Mustard or Mrs. Peacock or even for the demure Miss Scarlet. But they had some sense. The minute Dillworthy opened his mouth, they both fell asleep on the sofa. They didn't even have the energy to ask me to change the channel.

I studied the two men carefully. Hawthorne looked like a New England transcendentalist who got lost trying to find the twentieth century. His complexion was a sickly yellow and his lower lip had a peculiar self-righteous curl. There was something of the prig in the man but, I had to admit, something natural about him too. Decent. I didn't want to recognize that at first. It was too much of a shock to see it in a politician, an aberration of the human personality too extreme to trust—like meeting a bookie with a social conscience—but it was there all the same.

Dillworthy was something else again. His face was pan-
caked in layers, his hair lacquered and retouched follicle by
follicle. He must have spent more hours in make-up than
Gloria Swanson before she descended the staircase. He
looked like an interior decorator from a smallish Midwestern
city whose clients were beginning to desert him. He wanted
to win so badly he was constantly on the brink of tears, as
if the threat of an imminent emotional collapse in front of
millions of people would convince them to vote for him out
of a sense of priority. Don't let it come to this, folks. Don't
have my public breakdown on your shoulders . . . And when
he wasn't whining, he was flailing about in righteous in-
dignation, berating Hawthorne for anything his little mind
could think of. He would have accused him of pederasty
under the bleachers of Dodger Stadium, if he could have
gotten away with it.

But I wondered if he were capable of an act even more
desperate—if, like a Rotarian Richard III or a Kiwanis Club
MacBeth, he would drive for the throne along a grizzly trail
of blood.

I doubted it. He lacked the combination of determina-
tion and insanity necessary for such deeds. He was a sad
man when you thought about it, just barely hanging on. No,
it was likely someone else connected more tenuously to the
campaign.

I turned away from the television for a moment and
reached for the pamphlet listing the delegates. It was on the
couch under Jacob and I had to turn him on his side to get
it out. The pamphlet had been crumpled and the frontispiece
was torn. I flipped through the pages for the list of delegates
pledged to Governor Dillworthy. 238 names and then the
alternates. A long list of suspects and accomplices. The addresses were spread throughout the state—Marysville, Sac-
ramento, Petaluma, Oakland, San Bernardino, Bakersfield,
Stockton, Beverly Hills, Pasadena, San Pedro. And then

there were delegates and supporters from forty-nine other states. They were suspects too. The object of the smear was to win California, but that didn't mean the mastermind was a Californian. He could be from Illinois or Ohio or even Nevada.

I placed the pamphlet on the coffee table and returned to the debate. I would need more information before the names could mean anything. And the list didn't include financial backers, every one of whom had sufficient motive to shoot their mothers in the head with a burp gun, not to mention anything so mundane as pushing Lila Shea over a cliff after stashing a few reds in the glove compartment.

I took a second look at Hawthorne. He wasn't so different from Dillworthy. He wanted to win. Soothe his way into the soul of America like a man with his hand on his heart but his eyes cocked on McLuhan. I was rooting for him, rooting hard, but I wasn't sure I liked myself for it. Once you began to place your trust in a politician you were something of a fool. You ran the risk he would betray you for the next vote. And he surely would. He wouldn't have been there in the first place unless that was what he needed most of all. Politicians were like actors, always needing that external verification, as if life were one long instant replay in a world of Monday Morning Quarterbacks. Only actors sometimes improve with the feedback; politicians usually get worse.

A trio of CBS news men thanked the candidates and bid the nation goodnight. Jacob snorted through a stuffy nose like a rhinoceros with bronchitis. He was catching something and his little brother was soon to follow. I wrapped him in an afghan with a portrait of Trotsky in the middle that Aunt Sonya had knit and picked him up under my arm. What a load he was becoming. Then I propped Simon on my shoulder and headed out the door.

The night was cold and damp. The evening fog had

rolled in again from the ocean and I didn't notice the squad car blocking my driveway until I was halfway to the Buick. A plainclothes man and a driver were in the front seat. The plainclothes cop leaned out the window. He was smoking a rum crook and wearing a brown suit with thin 1958 lapels that looked like a Goodwill reject. The bashed-in Panama hat on his head I would have recognized anywhere.

"That you, Koontz?"

"Sure is, Wine. What're you doing here? The last plane for Peking left an hour ago."

"Very funny, Koontz. But this happens to be my house. And if you'll kindly move your ass out of the driveway. . . ." I continued past him and opened the door of my car.

"Just doing my job, Wine. Protecting you taxpayers. You do pay taxes, don't you?"

"Twice a day and a tithe to the Policeman's Retirement Fund."

"Oh, you've got a good sense of humor too, peeper." He flicked on his searchlight, beaming it into my eyes, then over the facade of the house. Jacob squinted and coughed a deep bronchial cough.

"I got a sick kid, Koontz," I said, putting the boys down carefully in the back seat. "You wouldn't want a case of pneumonia on your conscience."

He watched me for a moment. "There was a wreck up here a couple nights ago," he said.

I didn't say anything.

"Car went off the cliff. Looked like an accident but someone tipped us something else might be involved. . . . You know what I'm talking about?"

He beamed the light in my eyes again. I didn't give him the satisfaction of turning away.

"Sure you don't know what I'm talking about? I wouldn't like to see you get a blemish on your precious little detective's license."

45

"No idea."

He aimed the searchlight on the back of my car. I could hear the messages coming over the squawk box. A couple of hookers were picked up for loitering in front of the Hotel Cortes. Another full minute passed before the cop spoke again.

"Your left-turn signal's defective, Weinstein. You better have that fixed or you'll get yourself a citation." Then he tapped the driver on the shoulder and they took off.

I paused a few seconds before following them down the hill. If I knew Koontz, he'd be hiding in some cul-de-sac waiting to pick me up for doing 20 in a 30 zone, so I went around the long way through the winding streets on the far side of Elysian Park. It felt good when I reached the freeway and was out of his jurisdiction.

Back in Laurel Canyon, Suzanne was on the living room floor chanting a mantra with Madas. Both of them were wearing flimsy little white gowns. I could see her good breasts coming through the cotton.

8

N EXT MORNING I slept through the alarm. It was set for 7:30, but I pulled myself out of bed after 9:00 A.M. If I had dreams, I couldn't remember them. Without so much as a cup of coffee I got into my car and headed for East Los Angeles in search of Alora Vazquez.

Evergreen Way was one of those narrow rambling streets behind Brooklyn Avenue that resemble country roads more than the by-ways of a great metropolis. Much of East L.A. still looked like that, chickens running free in dirt alleys, corn growing helter-skelter in the front yards of ramshackle houses. You'd think you were in Mexico somewhere, a working-class barrio on the outskirts of Monterrey, until you reached the top of a hill and stared down at the civic center, its freeways interlacing high-rise office buildings like so many cement pretzels enclosing sterile glass monoliths.

A rundown synagogue stood at the corner of Evergreen and Soto, a testament to the former make-up of this community. I parked to the side where a swastika showed through a thick layer of whitewash. An orange van marked DOMESTIC SERVICES INC. drove past me, ferrying the "girls" to Beverly Hills. I got out of the car and proceeded up Evergreen to number 3201¼. It was a stucco court built around a row of banana trees but the leaves were all wilting and the trees were obviously on their last legs. Half the apartments in the court appeared to be either empty or unoccupied. I went around the back.

3201¼ was the smallest and most rundown of the lot. I was about to knock on the door when I saw Alora through the window, slipping on a white tee-shirt. She walked over to the mirror and began to brush her hair, pulling it back simply in a knot. Then she applied her make-up lightly. She didn't need it, but then it didn't hurt either. This girl would have looked good in a burlap bag with a hood over her head. Her high cheekbones were strong and Oriental like the Indian princesses in those sepia daguerreotypes of the Southwest. And the way her full ass pushed through the white linen pants, not even the great Quetzalcoatl himself could have planned it better.

She examined herself in the mirror for a final check, then went into the next room. I could hear her dialing a phone. I looked around the room. A frayed photograph was pinned to the wall near me. It showed a younger Alora with a boy who might have been her brother and a man who must have been their father, an aging *campesino* with one of those fine weathered Mexican faces that proved you could learn more from a year in the fields than ten in the library. But his daughter read too. A stack of tattered paperbacks reached the molding in the opposite corner of the room. From where I stood I couldn't read the titles.

It seemed peculiar a girl like this would be living in such a hovel. The walls were flaking and the carpets were threadbare. If the rent were more than thirty-five a month, it was highway robbery. Those Nevada hoods weren't treating her very well. They could have provided a room in a cheap motel. Then at least she'd have a free shoeshine cloth and television for a quarter a shot.

The phone clicked down and she came out of the back room, stopping to throw a denim jacket over her shoulder. I ducked behind the banana trees. Rather than confront her directly, I decided to let her lead me where I wanted to go.

She got into her Studebaker and proceeded down Evergreen past Soto, heading East. It was hard to tell whether she noticed me. I tried to stay a few blocks behind her, speeding up when she started up a hill so I wouldn't lose her at the top of a rise. But traffic on that back street was sparse, and we were often the only two cars on the road. At the corner of Evergreen and Lorena, she stopped for a red light. It was impossible for me not to pull up behind her. I flipped down my sun visor to make my face less visible and stared at the gas pedal waiting for her to start. She turned on Lorena and crossed Brooklyn to Fourth, turning once again beside a Catholic cemetery. I was at the top of a hill now and idled for a moment, allowing her to move ahead of me. But at the bottom she pulled into the parking lot of El Mercado, a large Mexican marketplace which took up a short city block between Lorena and Chicago Streets.

It was already mid-morning and the market was jumping like Monterrey on a Saturday night as I drove around the parking lot looking for a slot. They were hard to find and Alora was already long gone when I pulled in next to a Ford pickup. I could hear the screech of *mariachis* from the balcony above. I walked quickly across the lot to the front stairs and headed up, guessing that she was on the balcony. Upstairs, it was mobbed. The tables were jammed with Mexican families eating *gorditas* and fat green chili burritos. Little kids jumped around on the dance floor doing a four-year-old's version of La Bamba. Tough young machos stood by the foodstand with bottles of Dos X's in their hands, wearing skin-tight tee-shirts emblazoned with portraits of Zapata and Juarez. The girls circled around them in an endless *paseo* of tie-dyed capri pants and nylon tops cut at the midriff that would have struck terror in the heart of any *dueña* back in the old country. But then this wasn't the old country. El Mercado with its neon Pepsi signs and third-generation head shops mixed with fruit stalls and chili emporiums was part modern L.A., part funky Mexican but thoroughly Chicano. With the accent on the "cheek."

I made my own *paseo* around the balcony, stopping to peer into each of the little shops. I thought I saw Alora ducking through a beaded doorway, but it turned out to be the manicurist at the market barber shop. I continued on past the other stores, cutting through the magazine stand. The walls above the stand had been plastered with political posters aimed at garnering the Spanish-speaking vote. They showed Hawthorne with a variety of Mexican-American groups. *Hawthorne por la Causa. El Pueblo con Hawthorne. Cesar Chavez con Hawthorne.* On the other side of the stand, I came to the rail above the large produce market. Looking down, I was certain I could see Alora pushing a cart below.

I walked to the stairs and moved down swiftly. Keeping my distance, I could still see her in the spice department. She picked two different types of chili, then crossed over to the vegetables and examined the yellow jalapeño peppers, placing about a dozen in a brown paper bag. I moved closer, stopping at the end of the table. She turned and looked right at me, but seemed not to notice. At a table lined with greens—lettuce, parsley, and aromatic cilantro—she began to move more rapidly, wheeling her cart in front of her. I followed faster, trying not to attract the attention of the crowd. A Santana-like rock band had taken over for the mariachis. People were shouting and stomping to the rhythm of conga drums. It would be bad news indeed to be called attention to in this group. But she didn't appear to be yelling for help. She just walked quickly, up one aisle and down another, ignoring my presence.

Suddenly she abandoned her cart and left it in my path,

heading for the souvenir department. She began to run, through the sombreros and serapes and piles of ochre ceramics past the cheap Don Quixotes and velour bullfighters, in the direction of a side exit, pushing her way out. I reached the door seconds after her and grabbed the handle.

The first hit was smack on the jaw, the next right in the solar plexus, the third about three-quarters of an inch below my penis. Four or five faces swam in front of my eyes. A solid chop on the back of the neck and I plunged headfirst in a barrel of papayas. Then I heard a loud ringing noise that had nothing whatever to do with mariachis or Chicano rock or even a marimba band. It was more like an Anacin ad multiplied by a factor of two thousand, coupled with the uneasy feeling that my mouth had swallowed itself and that if I had any balls left I would have to forage for them the next morning among the garbage cans in the back of the market. Then I don't remember much of anything.

It might have been an hour, it might have been a week. Some light spilled in through the cracks in the shutters but there was no way of knowing what time of day it was. I tried to open my eyes wide but they would only go halfway before the lids started to throb. I touched my face and felt a banana-shaped welt swelling across the top of my forehead. My cheeks were scraped and covered with scabrous blood and my mouth was one long slice of putrified meat hung out like in *Potemkin* waiting for the maggots. I didn't dare find out if my teeth were still there. That could wait. My only consolation was that a good bash had straightened out the nose my mother had been badgering me about fixing all these years.

I rolled over on my side. I was on a mattress elevated a few feet off the ground in what seemed to be an abandoned warehouse. On a table in front of me were some colored objects made of papier-màché. With some difficulty I reached for one of them. It was a theatrical mask fashioned like an ancient Mexican god. I put it over my face and peered through the eyes, staring out into the darkness.

"Le gusta?" came a flat voice from across the warehouse.

I tried to sit up but fell back on my shoulder blades. The mask dropped to the floor.

"Perhaps you would like to join the *Teatro Comunal de Aztlan?*"

A ripple of laughter. There were others, maybe half a dozen.

I heard someone cross the room, then the lights were switched on. The glare of the exposed bulbs was strong. I threw my arm over my eyes.

More steps. I heard them circling around me.

"Where is Luis Vazquez?" came that voice again.

Who? What were they talking about? I tried to answer, but couldn't get anything together. Someone prodded me in the side with a sharp object.

"Where is Luis Vazquez?" said another voice.

I groaned, pulling the arm away from my eyes. There was a blur of brown faces in front of me. Over their heads I thought I recognized the insignia of the United Farm Workers: a black eagle on a red banner. My eyes closed.

"No contesta. . . . Let him sleep."

The lights went out and so did I.

Some time later they came on again. I could see clearly now, but my head still throbbed. About a dozen brown men and women stood in front of me wearing masks. One of them carried a guitar. The others were intertwined at the elbows, palms forward, linked together in theatrical poses. The group effect was a frieze, a *tableau vivant* drawn from a mural by Rivera, a fiesta on the Day of the Dead.

"Where is Luis Vazquez?" said the man with the guitar. His voice was becoming familiar.

"I don't know what you're talking about."

The five people in the front row threw back their robes, displaying machine guns. But I had to smile. They were obviously stage props.

"Where is Luis Vazquez?" "Where is Luis Vazquez?" "Where is Luis Vazquez?" One by one each of them spoke the words as if it were a litany. At last they came around to the man with the guitar again.

"Where is Luis Vazquez, anglo? You may find this amusing, but if he is dead, you will have to answer for it."

"I don't know who he is. I don't know where I am. I don't even know what day this is. Now if. . . ."

One by one again they removed the masks from their faces. The last was Alora.

"Where is Luis Vazquez, anglo?" she asked.

"Look. . . ."

"Where is he?"

A man by my head raised his stage machine gun and threatened to smash me in the mouth.

"Wait a minute! There's been a big mistake!" I tried to speak slowly, distinctly. "My name is Moses Wine. I'm a private detective, and I've never heard of Luis Vazquez."

"We don't believe you, anglo."

"You want proof, I. . . ." I reached for my wallet but of course it was gone. They smiled. The one with the guitar pulled it out from under his robe.

"Proof of what?"

I felt a sharp pain in my side as the machine gun came down.

"Lousy bastard," I muttered, loud enough to be understood. "Take out the address book. Turn to 'v.' Don Villarejo at the Barrio Defense League. He can vouch for me. . . ."

"Who?"

I felt another blow in the side.

"Don Villarejo. . . . You know Don Villarejo, don't you?"

They didn't answer.

On signal from the one with the guitar, they turned and, moving in an undulating pattern like a serpent, picked me up over their heads and carried me about the room. A man in the front clutched a real dagger in two hands as they chanted in some ancient tongue like Nahuatl. For a moment my sacrifice seemed a genuine possibility, even imminent. I saw visions of my bloody entrails pouring out over a giant calendar stone. But then, on another signal, I was replaced on the mattress and the lights were extinguished.

I lay back and tried to relax. In my present condition I wasn't prepared for this kind of exertion. I slept for a while, until I heard footsteps again. It must have been night because the light no longer leaked through the shutters. I sat up feeling an intense pain in my stomach as if my innards had been kicked upside down and were only now beginning to sort themselves out. I stared into the darkness looking for the troupe but there was only one person this time.

Alora lit the worklights and sat beside me on the edge of what I had come to realize was a stage. She was carrying a tray with a large bowl of soup and some surgical dressing.

"You should have told us," she said.

"What?"

"That you were the one who saved Alonso Alegria from a frame-up."

"He saved himself. The police didn't have a case." I rubbed my cheekbone where the rawness hurt. Off in an adjoining room, I could hear the one with the guitar singing a *corrido*. I couldn't make out all the words, but it was something about a young rebel in the Mexican Revolution who was a big hero until the government caught him in a cantina with the town whore and shot him dead.

"Still you should have told us," she said.

"You should have told me you had nothing to do with those Nevada punks."

Alora shrugged and ripped a piece of gauze along the seam, taping it to my cheek. "Take some menudo," she said, nodding toward the soup. It smelled good, but I wasn't ready to eat. My stomach would have rejected Simon's strained bananas.

"Who is Luis Vazquez?"

"My father, the founder of the *Teatro Comunal de Aztlan*."

"And why is he missing?"

"None of your business."

"Suppose I could help you find him . . . ?"

"You couldn't. And even if you could, it would still be none of your business."

"Why?"

"Because it is *una cosa de le Raza* . . ."

"Do you think he's alive?" I propped myself up on one elbow. For the first time I could make out the stage flats behind me. They were grape fields painted in perspective. Itinerant farm workers, tiny figures in white shirts and sombreros, were stretched out into the distance beneath a map of California, Arizona, New Mexico and parts of Northern Mexico. The word AZTLAN was stencilled across it.

Alora pushed me back on the mattress.

"Do I have to tell you again it's none of your business? I don't ask you why you were trailing me around El Mercado like a second-rate James Bond."

"Suppose I knew where you could find Luis Vazquez right now. Would you want to know?"

"Do you?"

"No."

"Then stop playing games."

I winced as she dug in her nails applying the dressing. She taped it, then moved her hands down my chest to where I had a large bruise around my abdomen. Her head was very close to mine and if I had leaned forward an inch our lips would have touched. I could feel my penis growing, and from the look on her face, it was obvious she noticed too.

"Una cosa Chicana," she reminded me, wrapping the gauze around my chest. Then she stood up and started to walk out. "Don't forget the menudo," she said. "If you let it get too cold, the fat congeals and floats to the top . . ." She flicked out the lights.

9

THE NEXT MORNING a man I hadn't seen before drove me back to El Mercado. He talked a blue streak about the boxing at the Olympic Auditorium. It seemed this Filipino had beat the shit out of the Nigerian champ in the bantam weights only the week before. The crowd was going wild. But wait until this guy met Jorge Orantes . . . fast, *por supuesto*, and born right here in the Barrio. Kick his ass.

We turned into the lot of El Mercado and I pointed out the Buick.

"That your short, man? . . . sheet!" We drove up and I got out. "You lucky to make it outta the lot."

"Thanks for the ride. Are you a member of the *Teatro Comunal de Aztlan*?"

"Hell no, man. Do I look like one of them actors? . . . *Maricones!* They jus' pay me a dollar to drive you over here."

"What happened to them?"

"They left for the *campo* . . . six o'clock this morning. . . . They do *actos* . . . little plays . . . for the people on the farm."

"I heard."

The driver backed his car, but stopped when his car came parallel to mine and rolled down the window. He had a pair of yellow tickets in his hand.

"Good seats, man. Third row. Orantes against that Filipino bastard. Gonna bust him good."

I shook my head.

Driving off, I turned on the radio to find out what day it was. Less than twenty-four hours had passed, but I had lost immeasurable time, gone up a false trail or at best a tangential one. The disappearance of Luis Vazquez seemed to have nothing to do with Howard Eppis on the face of it. And yet . . . Howard's path shouldn't have been that elusive. I was annoyed at my inability to track him down. Was it an omen that I shouldn't be looking in the first place or a sign hidden not far below the surface that I didn't really want to? I had phoned a few old political contacts but there were lots more I could have called. Was it just that I was ashamed to tell them that I was, in Sebastian's words, working within the system, supporting an Establishment politician? But they probably didn't care much for Eppis either. It was hard to figure.

When I reached my house, the phone was ringing. I ran to the door, but it had stopped before I entered and I continued on into the bathroom, stooping over the sink to wash. I peeled off the gauze Alora had taped to my cheeks and cleansed the bruises with rubbing alcohol while taking a long look at myself in the mirror. What a mess. I had barely crested thirty and my face already looked like the fag end of an Italian salami. The skin on my neck was ripped around the collar and dark purple bloodstains were spattered all over the front of my denim jacket. The plumbing in my house hadn't worked for months and I couldn't deposit the lousy three hundred bucks from the Hawthorne campaign for fear my creditors would attach my bank account. I closed my eyes. The throbbing had not gone away. If I had only stayed in law school I wouldn't be in this absurd condition. I'd be a nice young Jewish lawyer with a Matisse drawing on the office wall and twenty young draft dodgers as admirers. My wife wouldn't have walked out on me for some dimwit who can stick his right toe behind his left ear and my two boys would be right down the hall every night instead of in a canyon some three freeways away. I leaned down and spit in the sink.

The phone rang again. I wiped my hands on a towel and walked over to pick it up.

"Hello."

"Hello . . . Moses Wine?"

"Yes."

"This is Howard Eppis."

"Hello, Howard."

"I hear you wanted to talk with me."

The accent was nasal and New Yorky, the voice scratchy as if it were on a long distance line. But I couldn't be certain. Sometimes the corner druggist sounded like he was calling from Singapore.

"Are you close by?"

"Forget it, Wine. Say what you have to say over the phone or not at all."

I sat down on the couch, holding the telephone in my lap. The receiver felt clammy in my hand.

"Howard, do you want Hawthorne to win?"

"Sure."

"Some of his people don't think so."

"How's that?"

"Identifying a candidate with Mao and Lenin is worse than saying he had sodomy with the Pope. You don't need Gallup to tell you that."

"So what do they want me to do about it? Go play on the beach?"

"Stop sending those flyers, Howard."

A long silence from his end, then, "Not a chance!"

"You want to see Dillworthy win?"

Eppis laughed. "I didn't know Moses Wine was so concerned with the welfare of the Democratic Party."

He knew how to hurt.

"Look, Howard, why are you doing this? If you tell me your reasons, maybe we can work something out."

"I've my reasons for doing what I'm doing, Wine, and they're no concern of yours."

"What about Lila Shea?"

"Who?"

"Lila Shea."

"I haven't seen Lila in years."

"You won't have to. She went flying over the cliff on Cerro Gordo the other night."

A long pause. I stared into the mouthpiece of the phone, imagining Howard's grinning visage gone sour, his electric hair spraying out like a Medusa with a head full of Slinkys.

"You sure about that?" The voice was suddenly more timorous.

"Tell me your address and I'll send you the pictures."

"Jesus."

"You're being fucked over, Howard, by forces bigger than you."

"Her death didn't have anything to do with me."

"If I can prove it, will you stop what you're doing?"

"Go ahead and try, Moishe . . . but just warn your liberal pals over at Hawthorne Headquarters that the Free Amerika Party is going to be expressing its support for their candidate on a broad front and they better be prepared!"

"Where can I get ahold of you, Howard?"

"23 Columbia Drive."

He snickered and hung up.

Why had he called? I couldn't figure it, unless he was using me to put the knife to the Hawthorne people, possibly even set them up for some kind of blackmail. I decided to deliver the news to Sebastian in person. But on my way down Echo Park Boulevard, a squad car appeared in my rearview mirror. Within seconds the roof rotary was flashing. I pulled over into the discount gas station on the corner of Elmwood. A young Japanese cop got out of the car looking very businesslike.

"I know," I said. "The left-turn signal's not working."

He didn't respond, checking some information on a clipboard instead. "Moses Wine?" I nodded. "Follow me, please?"

"What's this about, officer?"

"Detective Koontz of the Rampart Division wants to speak with you."

"Oh, yeah. And suppose I don't want to speak with him?"

"Then a warrant will be issued."

Simple enough.

The cop got back in his squad car and I followed him down to Alvarado, turning right on Temple Street to the Rampart Division, a depressing edifice squatting between a Cuban restaurant and a laundromat. The facade was an endless slab of grey cement surrounding an equally endless collection of grey minds. I parked in a slot marked visitors and went up the steps to the main lobby. Koontz was waiting for me in a back office with a stenographer. He was in bad need of a shave and his shirt looked like it just came from a steam pressing in the tail pipe of a garbage truck. As usual, his panama hat was so bashed in you couldn't tell whether it was upside down or not.

"Call off your goons, Koontz." I pointed to the stenographer. "This isn't the line-up."

"I thought you might want to make a statement."

"About what?"

"About the so-called accident on Cerro Gordo."

"What accident?"

"The one in which a twenty-eight-year-old woman went over a cliff."

"You're wasting your time, Koontz. You should be out there doing something constructive like collecting graft or shaking down a homosexual."

"We'll see about that," he said, sounding cocky. He reached inside his desk and brought out a file labelled WINE, Moses S. The name had a familiar ring to it. "Do you know a Miss—or should I say Ms.—Lila Shea?"

The stenographer began to copy the question at a furious clip. "Get him out of here," I said. "Or I'll have to call my lawyer. You know us Jews, Koontz. We all have smart lawyers with big vocabularies."

Koontz didn't smile. But he beckoned with his head to the stenographer, who got up and left. Then he opened my file and began to thumb through it. It appeared to have grown since the last time I was there.

"Do you know a Lila Shea?" he repeated.

"I couldn't say."

"What do you mean, you couldn't say?" He waited a split second for a reaction. "She was the one who went off Cerro Gordo at 1:45 the morning of May 24, precisely .07 miles from your house. . . . Does that refresh your memory?"

"Interesting."

"Is that all?" He was beginning to smirk. He removed the top sheet from my folder and placed it beside the active file to his right, reading from the top, "Item—Lila Shea. UC Berkeley, 1964, BA in English. Item—Moses S. Wine. UC Berkeley, 1963, BA in English."

"Two English majors . . . remarkable."

"Item—Lila Shea: member, Fair Play for Cuba Committee; member, Committee to Free Caryl Chessman. Item—Moses S. Wine: member, Fair Play for Cuba Committee; member, Committee to Free Caryl Chessman."

"Fascinating coincidence. . . ."

He held up a photograph. "Item—Lila Shea *and* Moses Wine. Bay Area March to Ban the Bomb, March 1962."

I looked at the picture. The framing wasn't bad but the focus was lousy. Lila and I were circled with a grease pencil. There were about six demonstrators between us.

"Do you deny you know Lila Shea?"

"I don't deny it." I looked out the window hoping flying saucer would swoop down on Temple Street and carry me off to a distant planet. But that only happened in Vonnegut novels. 'I don't confirm it, either."

"You wouldn't." He replaced the documents in my file and leaned back, staring at me for a minute. "What happened to your face, Wine? You look like you fell off a cliff yourself."

"I got into a fast poker game with three Arabs and a Greek. They wouldn't believe it when I drew four kings."

He sat up straight. "All right. Cut the shit. Who is she? Who're you working for and what're you doing?"

I preened my hair.

"Get smart, Wiener. I've got enough on you to drop your license in a vat of sulphuric acid and throw away the rubber gloves. I could drive up to your house right now and bust you for enough drugs to send you to Soledad until the mid 1980's. Now who're you working for and what's going on?"

"You should know that, Koontz."

"What do you mean, I should know?!"

"You've got my whole life on file. You probably were tapping my mother's phone when she called her sister from the maternity ward."

"Are you going to cooperate, or . . ."

"And violate my client's confidence? What do you think?"

"Get lost," he said. I stood to leave but he stopped me at the door. "Just remember one thing, peeper. Our informant tells us he saw you with Miss Shea on the night of her death. That makes you our only suspect."

"Tell your informant he's a creep." I opened the door and left.

10

I DROVE HOME wondering who his informant was and how he or she fit into the puzzle with Alora, Eppis and Lila Shea. Or if there was a puzzle ... if, indeed, they were all related. And what of Luis Vazquez. This whole affair was turning into one dense sea of missing persons and I was about as close to the bottom of it as a scuba diver at the edge of the Barrier Reef. And now with Koontz sticking his stuffy nose into things. . . .

When I got home, I went directly to the closet. The hash was still in its place hidden in the toes of my smelly tennis sneakers and the Michoacan remained unmolested in the canister labelled Dunhill My Mixture No. 1275. I thought of throwing it all down the toilet but then life is short and what's a few years in the cooler for possession. I'd miss the boys but at least I'd never have to lay eyes on that jerk Madas again.

I sat down at the Clue set for a while and fiddled with the pieces. But real life had taken over from the game and the evil doings of Colonel Mustard & Co. just didn't seem interesting. I picked up the list of delegates again, flipping through it for inspiration. Then I rifled the pages of *Rip It*

Off. Nothing. I lay back and had one of my least favorite fantasies—that private investigation was an imbecile's job and anybody could do it. Things that got solved, got solved. And things that didn't, didn't. Either information floated to the surface or it never came. All you needed was a fool there who could catch it.

I walked over to the refrigerator, and made myself three tuna fish sandwiches on rye, a homage of sorts to the memory of Lila Shea. Then I ate a couple of tortillas with butter and salt, a salute to Alora. Maybe I'd see her again some time. I checked the clock: 4:15. Still early enough to get down to Hawthorne Headquarters and report Eppis' words to Sebastian. It was, after all, what they paid me for.

As a precaution against police surveillance, I did not head directly for the headquarters but drove down to Sunset and parked in the lot of Anchors Away!, a schlock import store of maddening proportions. Milling with the crowds of bargain-hunters, I entered the store and headed for the rear exit, slipping out behind a man carrying a pair of rattan bar stools from Mali and a large bolt of sackcloth from a Micronesian island with an unpronounceable name. I continued on foot for several blocks to Vermont and took a bus from there to Hawthorne Headquarters. When I arrived, the precinct workers were returning from their rounds. I watched them deliver their portfolios to a tall black woman who inspected the computer read-outs, checking off their names on a legal-sized pad. The volunteers compared notes and swapped stories of their various assignments with a feeling of camaraderie.

"Five times I knocked," a college kid was saying. "Finally this bastard opens the louvres and shoves a shotgun right in my ear. . . . I put him down as 4, very unfavorable."

I edged my way around the receptionist's desk but was stopped by a hand on my shoulder. It was Sugars. He was in his shirtsleeves with hair hanging over his forehead in a contrived Bobby Kennedy style.

"What're you doing here?" He greeted me like an escapee from a leper colony.

"I've got to talk with Sebastian. It's important."

"Sebastian's not here."

"When's he coming back?"

"A couple of days. I sent him down to Bakersfield to do some advance work."

"You?"

"I'm with the national campaign. He's with the state campaign. That gives me seniority."

The elevator opened and he moved toward it, a man on his way to important meetings in the executive suites. I moved fast to keep up with him.

"Eppis called," I told him.

Sugars didn't respond.

"He may be trying to set you up. Blackmail of some sort."

He reached the elevator and stopped, blocking the door with his foot.

"Look, Wine, do yourself a favor. If you want to stay on the payroll, keep far away from here. There's nothing Eppis can do to us now. He's not big enough. But the police already have your name in connection with a murder and you can smear us good."

He ducked inside the elevator and pressed the button. In a moment the door closed about his corpulent body. I turned around and stared at a large bulletin board. It contained a bar graph showing the relative strength of the candidates over the last few months according to an unspecified poll. Hawthorne's popularity was soaring. There was no doubt he would smash Dillworthy. They couldn't stop him now, not even if a CBS mobile unit caught him jacking off on the roof of the Union Bank Building with an old Brownie shot of Pat Nixon. Or so it seemed.

I walked back through the reception room past walls papered with ecology symbols in pastel colors. The Osmond Brothers came from a loudspeaker at a discreet volume. On my left, the volunteers were seated at long camp tables as busy as ants in one of those glassed-in colonies you buy on television. Strolling idly through the room, I felt out of place, at odds with my environment, the last hold-out for alienation in a world of engaged men.

"Hey . . . just a minute!" A girl stopped me as I tried to walk into the corridor between the county and state head-quarters. "You can't go in there without a pass!"

"Right arm," I said, holding up my palm like Dave Garroway on the *Today* show years ago, and walked out of the building.

It was still light when I got back to my car at the Anchors Away! parking lot. I drove out onto Sunset and headed for Venice to have another look at 23 Columbia Drive. Perhaps Eppis' last words to me were no more than frivolity, but I didn't have enough leads to be choosy.

I reached the cul-de-sac just as the sky turned pitch dark. Driving around the loop, I was surprised to find that number 23 had been leveled in its entirety. The faded Victorian mansion had disappeared, leaving only a vacant lot with a new sign from Pacific Properties listing its dimensions, 175' × 115'. I parked around the corner and got out, pausing only to pick my flashlight out of the glove compartment. The street was empty except for the abandoned shell of a Chevy convertible at the far end. Over on the next block I could see the neon sign of a soul food restaurant flashing on and off.

I crossed the street quickly, continuing along the sidewalk past the now-vacant lot to the house with the Venetian blinds. It was pink stucco with a red tile roof and a large metal alarm box that any self-respecting burglar would know was a phony. I rang the buzzer. In a few seconds a dark brown eye appeared in the peephole.

"Who is it?" came a woman's voice.

"Moses Wine, ma'am. I'm an investigator."

The eye turned away. "It's the welfare investigator, Harry."

"Tell him to go away," replied a man.

I knocked on the door. "I'm not the welfare investigator, ma'am. I'm a private detective. I'd like to speak with you for a moment."

I took out my wallet and held up my license, as if that proved anything. She opened the door a crack. I saw an elderly Filipino woman in her housecoat. In the kitchen behind her, her husband was eating his supper, some sort of noodle dish. He wore a hearing aid.

"What's this about?"

"Sorry to interrupt your dinner, ma'am. It's about the place next door . . . the one that was levelled." I tried to enter the house, but she kept her foot firmly against the door.

"Tell him to go away," her husband repeated without bothering to look up from his dinner.

"He's not the welfare investigator, Harry," she shouted to him. "It's about the place next door."

"What?"

"The place next door!"

"Oh."

He finished chewing his food. Then, slowly, something dawned on him. He began to grin, turned and walked over to me. "Batman!" he said, flapping his wings like a reject from the corps de ballet.

"He's crazy," said the wife. "Always seeing things. He's very sick."

"I am not!" said the man, suddenly able to hear perfectly well.

She turned toward him angrily: "Go finish your dinner!" I seized the moment to take a couple of steps inside the house. It was furnished plainly. A big Motorola color TV stood by the bedroom door beneath a travel poster of Okinawa.

"There was never anyone in that house," she told me. "It's been empty for years."

"Nonsense," he yelled at her, still dancing about the room. "You always go to sleep at nine o'clock. They don't come until twelve . . . one in the morning."

"Who doesn't come?" I asked him.

"Strange characters," he said, his eyes twinkling like an old Oriental storyteller. "Big black cape and red boots. Fancy clothes and make-up like women of the streets . . . but witches. You know what I mean?"

I nodded my head like I knew what he meant. "Did they come often?"

"One, maybe two times. Late at night."

"Where'd they go?"

"Down the back stairs. With candles. Like this." He held his hands wide to indicate a candelabra. His wife shook her head in disgust.

"Did you see what they did?"

"I ne—"

"Quiet, Harry!" she interrupted. "You're talking nonsense."

He waved her off. "I never saw anything except one time." His wife looked away in irritation. "In back of house . . . King Nestor hit the witch girl with a silver stick. Phew! Lots of blood."

"King Nestor?"

"The man with the cape. Batman! That's what they called him."

"How do you know that?"

I waited for an answer but he just laughed and waved at me and headed back into the kitchen.

"What about a tall blonde woman?" I asked. "Or a guy with hair out to here. . . . real wiry?"

But he didn't appear to be listening. He sat down at the table to resume his meal. Then the wife came over and put her hand on my arm with a grave expression.

"It's hard for me," she said, "taking care of him. He never remembers where he is. He's senile." I nodded to her and started out the door, but she caught my arm again. "Listen, mister, you're a private detective. My husband's brother in San Francisco . . . he owes us $235 for seven years and he won't pay. Can you make him give it back?" She held tight to my arm, placing her forehead very close to mine. Her pupils appeared exceptionally large behind thick bifocals.

"Sorry," I said, pulling free and slipping out the door.

The night was cool and damp from the ocean. I walked over to the lot. It was practically barren. All I could see from the sidewalk were some asbestos shingles piled to the side and the upended remnants of a toilet seat. I flicked on the flashlight and beamed it about the ground. The basement had been excavated, leaving only the bare bones of the foundation, a few concrete walls and the pilings. I jumped down, shining the flashlight on the cement. A well-fed rat darted across the floor and into a hole in front of me. Moving forward, I walked along the basement wall. At eye level I spotted a pile of rubble at the end of the property.

I clambered out again and walked over, inspecting the debris. Most of the mound consisted of caked mud and broken pieces of concrete, but near the bottom I saw the edge of something more brightly colored sticking out from under a coffee tin—a shard of ceramic stuck in the moist earth. I dug it out with a sharp rock. A five-pointed star was drawn carefully on the surface, in the center of a circle with two points at the top. A goat was in the center and Hebrew letters appeared at the tip of each point. It was nearly twenty years since my Bar Mitzvah and I couldn't make it out. I put the fragment in my pocket and headed for the car. Off in the distance I could see the old man standing at the Venetian blinds, watching.

11

Late next morning I went down to Barney's Voodoo Store, a large magic shop on Hollywood Boulevard between a reducing salon and a lingerie boutique catering to topless dancers and transvestites. When I arrived, the salesmen were all occupied with kids buying itching powder and invisible ink. I waited by a shelf lined with cardboard boxes of miniature Egyptian mummies until the first one was free.

"What's this?" I asked, passing the fragment over to a tall man with a Walter Matthau stoop. He held it in his right hand, scrutinizing it closely and rubbing his chin with the back of his left. He had a heavy five-o'clock shadow.

"The Pentagram of Solomon," he replied, watching me. "Very rare . . . very rare indeed."

"What does it do?"

"Wards off evil spirits. This one, of course, is upside down in the Satanist manner."

"What about the animal in the middle?"

"The Witches' Sabbath. The goat. An excellent symbol."

"I'm sure," I said. "Who do you think would have one of these?"

"Only the truly enlightened."

"Naturally."

"They're almost impossible to find." The salesman leaned in toward me out of the eager hearing range of a six-year-old girl dangling a rubber spider. "But," he continued, "we at Barney's have a few left, just a few, at $17.95 plus five percent for that mean man in Sacramento." He eyed me carefully, waiting for my response. "We also have exclusive Satan cocktail napkins with the inverted cross at $7.50 the dozen. A great conversation stimulus."

I begged off and headed for the door. It was already eleven-thirty and I wanted to speak with Earl Speidel.

I found him over lunch at Geronimo's Gardens, a favorite gathering place of record-business types featuring a large papier-mâché sculpture of Geronimo surrounded by palm fronds. Earl was seated with Johnny Pace, the publicity director of Grit Records, a skinny amphetamine addict in a suede suit and yellow sunglasses.

"King Nestor?" Earl shook his head in amusement. "Sounds like a new breakfast cereal. King Nestor, the sugar-frosted treat. And it's chock full of vitamins and minerals, too."

"What about 23 Columbia Drive?"

"Means nothing to me."

"Then how about this?" I removed the fragment from a brown paper bag and handed it to him. He examined it without a great deal of curiosity.

"What is it?" he asked.

"The Pentagram of Solomon. Wards off evil spirits. Or in this case welcomes them . . . $17.95 at Barney's." He didn't respond. "Ever see one before?"

"How should I know? A record jacket for Black Sabbath?"

"Very funny. What about Procari? Did he ever have one of these?"

"Procari had everything but the Bhagavad-Gita in Yiddish. You're not interested in Procari, are you?"

I took the fragment away and put it back in the bag. A waiter came up to take my order.

"Try the organic maize," said the super duper. "It's made from an original Sioux recipe!"

"Give me a BLT down and a Seven-Up. . . . Easy on the mayonnaise." The waiter left with a sullen expression. "Tell me about Procari, Earl. You said they never found evidence of his death."

"I didn't say that. They found pieces of his car—the Maserati—a silk scarf he always wore and his goddamn bones for crissake. The way he used to drive around, I wouldn't doubt he could fly off a cliff at Palos Verdes. No one could come out of there alive. You know the place."

I nodded. An image of rocks jutting out into the Pacific flashed through my mind. Deadman's Curve. It had earned that nickname a few years ago when a trio of bikers, high on reds, pushed a young woman in a Fiat over the apron and into the ocean. Minutes later the bikers flew over it themselves, chased in the opposite direction by the police.

"But you mentioned something about his old followers still being convinced he's alive."

"Well, sure. Every cult's got its die-hard devotees, doesn't it? Jesus is alive and well in Butte, Montana. James Dean has reappeared as a dentist in Sydney, Australia. Bird lives. You name it."

"Who are they? Do you remember any of them specifically?"

"His biggest booster was this woman Isabel La Fontana. I think she lives in the Hollywood Hills someplace in a Norman-style building with a moat and a couple of German shepherds with filed teeth. They wrote her up a few years ago in an Esquire article on California witchcraft. I remember a photo of her in white make-up and claw-like finger-nails painted black."

"Isabel La Fontana, that's a stage name, isn't it?"

"How the hell should I know? She used to do a nightclub act back in the fifties, kind of an incestuous thing with her son."

"Dynamite," Pace said, clapping his hands together. "Hey, what's this about, guys? Anything old Johnny should know?"

"Not if I can help it," I said, leaving a couple of bills on the table for my uneaten BLT. I threaded my way through Geronimo's Gardens and out into the parking lot. My decrepit Buick was wedged tightly against a 1932 Duesenberg, but I managed to squeeze it out without chipping any of the precious paint.

An hour later, armed with a frayed copy of the May 1970 *Esquire*, I climbed up Kings Way to the Hollywood Hills home of Isabel La Fontana. But when I got there, I was puzzled with what I found. She lived in an imitation Norman castle, all right, but Isabel herself was a far cry from the Slinky Queen of the Night. Instead I saw a tired, pasty-faced woman some twenty years beyond the thirty-one ascribed to her by Esquire, with vague alcoholic eyes that didn't always focus. When I crossed the tiny drawbridge leading to her front door, she was sitting in her faded pastel bermudas with her feet dangling among the goldfish in the moat, tossing dog bisquits to two panting German shepherds. The dogs greeted me with friendly yips and shy licks at the palm of the hand. Times had changed, Isabel readily explained as I followed her into the castle. A few years ago Satanism was all the rage. Then along came Esalen with encounter groups, nude therapy, rolfing, that kind of thing. People were mixed up. Misled. They didn't realize the Devil was more than just another kookie Southern California fad.

The furnishings were a testament to the erosion of Isabel's empire. The castle was filled with a mélange of imitation medieval bric-a-brac and the harsh synthetic furniture available at wholesale houses, the kind that looked great until the first cup of spilled coffee filtered through the fabric and rusted out the springs. My guess was that the better pieces had already been repossessed. We sat down on a Herculon couch opposite a wall of photographs of Isabel with various local celebrities. I recognized the former star of a TV situation comedy and the well-known owner of a chain of used car lots.

"Aren't there any Satanists left?" I asked.

"A few. The sincere ones." She fixed me in her alky gaze, as if sizing me up as a future convert. "What paper did you say you were with, Mr. Wine?"

"The *L.A. Bat*, the underground newspaper."

"Oh, the *Bat*!" she exclaimed. "I love their classified advertisements ... the personals column especially." She paused while I took out a pad and paper. "People are so honest about their needs in it. And I don't believe any of us should be ashamed of our needs. Do you, Mr. Wine?"

"Not at all," I said, noticing for the first time the thin pencil scar beneath her chin, the sure sign of a recent face lift. She rested her hand on my knee.

"Tell me, Miss La Fontana, who do you regard as some of the more significant figures in the Satan Movement over the last few years?"

"Well," she said, leaning in closely. "Let me say straight off that Charlie Manson was a phony through and through. Not an authentic Satanist. He gave us a bad name."

"Did you have any true leaders?"

"The Fallen Angel is our true leader," she said gravely, taking me by the hand. "What is it that Milton wrote? 'To do aught good never will be our task,/But ever to do ill our sole delight.' ... Would you like something to drink? A brandy?"

I nodded and she poured us both a drink from a plastic flask on the end table.

"To the Underworld," she said, "and the Children of Darkness," as we clicked glasses. I resisted a smile and drank, wondering whether it contained the juices of the poisonous mandrake root or some other bizarre potion. It tasted like cheap brandy.

"Then you haven't had any secular leaders in recent years," I said.

"Well, of course we've had some. Lemuel Fleet in San Francisco. Roger Hendricks, an expert in necromancy and the four cardinal points. Norbert Hertside, the Caballist." She brought my hand to her lips and blew softly. "And there are those who consider me one of the leaders of our sect. . . . Have you ever made love with your hands manacled to a post, Mr. Wine?"

"Not while I was awake."

"You should try it." She clasped both her hands around mine and squeezed with great urgency. For a fleeting moment, despite her decay or maybe because of it, I felt the power she must have had. Or still had for all I knew. "Our beliefs aren't as foolish as you might think," she continued. "Remember the Manichean heresy, the forces of light and darkness grappling in all of us . . . in you right now. You will write good things about us in your newspaper, won't you? We need your help."

"Sure . . . look . . . I, er, would like to attend a Black Mass." She smiled, pleased with the request. "You think it would be possible for me to attend one with King Nestor?"

She dropped my hand instantly and drew back, eyeing me with tremendous suspicion.

"Who told you about him?"

"Everybody knows about King Nestor," I tried.

"They do?"

"He's Oscar Procari, Jr., isn't he? The son of the famous financier."

"Oscar Procari is dead. He died two years ago in an automobile accident."

I looked at her wide-eyed. "Are you sure?"

"Oscar Procari is dead," she repeated. "You can read about it yourself in the newspapers."

"Gee," I said. "Someone told me he was still alive. That he didn't want to expose himself for fear the wrong parties would take advantage of him."

"That someone was misinformed." She stood and stepped away from the couch.

"If he isn't Procari, then who is he?"

"You may leave now, Mr. Wine."

"But the interview has only begun. I have so many questions. . . . Did I say anything wrong?"

"You'd better leave."

I ignored her request and walked over to a brass-framed photograph of a man in a black hood leading a ritual of some sort. A nude woman lay on a slab in front of him with a snake crawling up her stomach.

"Is that him? Is that Procari?"

"I said go, Mr. Wine."

"Why're you afraid to tell me? I don't understand."

"King Nestor has powers none of us can fathom." She headed for the opposite side of the room. "He is the hope of our movement."

"Then he is alive!" I said, following after her.

But she didn't reply. Instead she slid her hand beneath a mirror, switching off the chandelier and leaving one lone candle flickering on the mantelpiece. The room became quite dim. I hadn't realized it was without windows. Then she reached down to her right and picked up a large leather whip, cracking it sharply over my head. The two German shepherds appeared at the entrance of the foyer. This time they weren't the amiable pets that had greeted me at the front door. Growling ominously, they seemed like a pair of refugees from the guard tower at Bergen-Belsen with a couple of my ancestors sloshing about in their bellies. In the faint light, Isabel herself, even with pastel bermudas and bleary alcoholic eyes, had taken on the imposing aspect of her old *Esquire* spread. And the whip she held in her hand didn't help matters. She looked like she knew how to use it.

"Do you have any more questions, Mr. Wine?" Her voice had become constricted, distant.

"No, no. I don't think so." I was surprised at my own docility. I tried to laugh, but it didn't seem very funny.

"Then our interview is over."

"Yes." I nodded and she guided me to the foyer with the dogs trailing a few feet behind us.

She touched my leg with the whip in farewell. "I'll be looking forward to your article, Mr. Wine. The *Bat* has always been one of my favorite newspapers."

In a moment I was out on the street. The sun was blinding. I turned back to the house. The few slatted windows were all shuttered. I could hear the dogs barking from within the thick Norman ramparts. They were probably ripping apart a piece of lean red sirloin steak. It would make a diverting spectacle but I had no inclination to go back and watch.

12

THE OCCULT IS about ninety-five per cent sham, I thought that night as I packed my pipe with as much hashish as I could possibly cram in the bowl, but that other five per cent could sure scare the shit out of you. I took a good heavy toke and held it in as long as I could, trying to dissolve the wave of paranoia which had engulfed me ever since I left Isabel La Fontana's. In a short time I was feeling somewhat better. Perhaps I had been smoking too much dope of late but I consoled myself that I hadn't yet passed Sherlock Holmes who, in *The Sign of Four*, took three cocaine injections a day and lay upon his sofa "for days on end . . . hardly uttering a word or moving a muscle from morning to night."

I lay back on my own and lifted over my head the photocopies of 1970 newspaper articles I had made at the downtown library that afternoon.

Palos Verdes Estates, May 17—Citizens of this wealthy suburb were treated to a terrifying spectacle last night as a flaming Maserati Coupe smashed through the barricade near

Cohelan Drive and the Pacific Highway and plunged into the ocean.

The vehicle was owned by Oscar Procari, Jr., of West Hollywood, a self-described priest in the Church of the Five Deities. Mr. Procari was said to have been driving the car at the time of the accident.

I flipped the page.

Palos Verdes Estates, May 19—Police are finding it difficult to make a positive identification of the driver incinerated in the crash of a Maserati in the Pacific near Cohelan Drive three nights ago. Both car and driver were badly fragmented, suggesting a gas explosion while the car was still in the air, police say.

I turned to the next one.

Palos Verdes Estates, May 20—Police now have definitely identified the victim in the May 16 Maserati crash here as Oscar Procari, Jr., the vehicle's owner.

Identification was aided by members of Procari's Church of the Five Deities who provided authorities with X-rays of the victim. The coroner's office was then able to compare the deceased's bone structure with the few remaining fragments.

It seemed possible that "King Nestor" was the reincarnation of Procari, a code name of sorts to disguise a reappearance that might have been planned as long as two years ago. But reappearance for what? To defeat the candidacy of Miles Hawthorne? It didn't make sense. Hawthorne wasn't even a candidate at that time. To take over a burgeoning Satan cult in Southern California? Surely that had backfired.

I thumbed through the articles again, then placed them on the table next to the list of delegates and a copy of *Rip It Off*. How did Howard fit in with this? For all his pathetic qualities, his ersatz radicalism, it was still depressing to imagine him so brainwashed by a devil cult he would adhere to their every wish, even if that meant looking the other way from murder.

I got up and put on a pot of espresso from the Cuban grocery store down the street. The night was still young and maybe if I plowed my way through Aleister Crowley's *Magick in Theory and Practice*, I could figure out what they were up to. Or perhaps if I got super-stoned and hallucinated my way into Goya's illustrations of the Witches' Sabbath. Or better yet, I could take a ride over to Pacific Properties and beat up Flint. But that might just get me a piece of Nestor's silver stick in the back of my neck. Then the phone rang.

"Hello, Wine." It was Sebastian.

"Hello, Sam. How's Bakersfield?"

"Was Bakersfield . . . I just got back. I heard you were in touch with Eppis."

"Yeah, I—"

"It can keep. Something really urgent came up. Can you get away?"

"Sure, I'll be right there."

"No, not here. It's too risky. I'll be in the parking lot of Tiny Naylor's in half an hour."

I got there ahead of him and waited in the Buick with the motor running. Bleach blonde waitresses shimmied from car to car taking orders for chili burgers and fries from teenagers in shiny Bonnevilles with spurs. It was like a Chamber of Commerce picture of California in the fifties. Only now the waitresses needed bridge work and most of the teenagers were drag queens.

Sebastian arrived on foot. He didn't say anything but beckoned for me to follow him across the parking lot in the direction of the Carolina Pines Motel. When we reached the sidewalk on Highland Avenue, he pointed to a white Mercury Cougar parked in front of the motel. We got in and headed off on Sunset going west. After about half a mile, he took a letter out of his pocket and handed it to me. It was neatly typed on the kind of plain stationery available at any five and ten cent store.

To the So-Called Liberals at Hawthorne HQ:

Be advised the Free Amerika Party plans its greatest demonstration of support for Senator Miles Hawthorne early the morning of May 31, 1972. At that time the whole nation—probably even the whole world—will know we're behind Senator Hawthorne. So just remember, stay clear of Harbor, Hollywood and San Bernardino Freeways—that is, if you value your own life.

Yours for the victory in the primary and
victory in November,
H. Eppis

It was postmarked Pomona, California, May 27 and addressed to Mr. Sam Sebastian, County Coordinator, Hawthorne Headquarters, 4901 Wilshire Boulevard.

"He means to blow up a freeway, doesn't he?" said Sebastian.

"I don't think he wants to lead the parade."

"What are you going to do about it?" He stopped for a red light at the corner of Sunset and Fairfax.

"I don't know."

"What do you mean you don't know?! You've got some leads, haven't you?"

I nodded. The light changed and we continued up Sunset past the Directors' Guild and the Bank of America.

"What have you got?"

"Nothing much. A Satan cult."

"A Satan cult?" He sounded annoyed.

"A faded Satan cult. Passé. They operated out of a recording studio in Westwood. After that they were on Columbia Drive."

"That doesn't make sense. Why would Satanists care about an election?"

But I wasn't listening. "Turn left!" I said.

"What?"

"Turn left!" I grabbed his shoulder. "We're being followed!"

He seemed confused. I reached over him and twisted the wheel, turning us off onto Crenshaw Boulevard.

"Now double back."

"What?"

"Double back!" I shouted. "Don't you speak English?"

I looked out the rear window. The green Chevy with the Nevada plates was fifty yards behind us.

"Who's that?" Sebastian asked.

"I don't know."

"Then how do you know they're following us?"

"Don't worry about it. Just turn." I pulled the steering wheel again and we went off on Santa Monica past Tana's Restaurant and the Troubadour. Then up Doheny at about eighty miles per hour. Sebastian hunched over the wheel with a grim expression on his face. The guys in the Chevy were good. They stayed right behind us.

"Now there," I said, pointing at a side street which wound up into the hills behind the Whiskey-A-Go-Go. "Step on it!" I pressed my foot over Sebastian's on the gas pedal to give him a little extra encouragement. Soon we were up over the city, tearing across Mulholland Drive with our tires screeching like wounded hyenas. The lights of L.A. stretched out in front of us, a rhinestone paradise.

Then we drove down again, into Laurel Canyon, dark with ominous eucalyptus trees hovering above us. A trio of hitch-hikers appeared momentarily at the side of the road and Sebastian nearly swiped them.

"Having fun?" I asked.

"We're not losing them," he said. "Where're we headed?"

"Just drive."

We sped past the Canyon Store and Cafe Galleria. Traffic was picking up in the opposite direction, people returning to the Valley after a night on the town. A police helicopter dropped into the canyon, shining its beacon on the passing cars, and then disappeared again. I tugged on Sebastian's arm.

"Slow down."

He eased up on the accelerator.

"There."

I aimed my index finger at a bright fluorescent sign, black against white lettering: Mt. Olympus. A small fountain played in front of it, illuminated with a pink spotlight. We turned up the hill behind it, twisting back and forth on narrow roads with names like Zeus Way and Athena Drive. The empty streets were lined with newly-planted cypresses and Italian pines. Hundreds of sites had been levelled, sliced like miniature landing strips in the side had been of the mountain, but remained unbuilt, a financial disaster.

"Higher," I said, urging him on. The green Chevy was on the hill beneath us, only two switch-backs behind. Continuing ahead, we came to a roundabout at the top. Olympus Circle. A bulldozer stood by the apron in front of the facade of a half-finished French Provincial mansion.

"Pull over."

"I hope you know what you're doing."

"Run down that embankment and come back in ten minutes." We both got out of the car. But Sebastian didn't move. He just stood there in a daze. "Get going," I said.

He nodded and started running down the incline behind the facade of the mansion. At the same moment I could see the Chevy coming up to his left. I climbed into the bulldozer and slumped down to eye level.

In a few seconds the Chevy drove into the circle, moving slowly. It came up behind Sebastian's car, giving it the once-over, then came around to my side. I could see the two men well now. Both of them were burly types, short-haired Marines, with banlon shirts, beige and brown. The one who wasn't driving carried a snub-nosed Saturday Night Special close to chin level. They drove around a couple of more times, talking to each other, obviously trying to decide if we were still nearby. At length they pulled over by a pile of two-by-fours. The driver got out and stood in front of his car while his mate proceeded in the direction of the French Provincial facade. When he reached the door, he grabbed the handle and pulled it open. Through the frame the lights of West Hollywood stretched off into the distance. He stepped past and disappeared out of sight.

Slowly, silently, I lowered myself out of the bulldozer. I could see the driver's trouser legs. Keeping my eye on him, I crept around the side of the vehicle. He leaned back on the hood of the Chevy. I didn't have a plan really, but when I got up close to him, I leapt out and grabbed the bastard by the neck, squeezing for all I was worth. We fell to the ground and rolled over to the gutter.

"Lila Shea, you fucker. Lila Shea," I shouted. I found myself smashing his face, gouging my knee into his kidney. "Who killed Lila Shea?"

"I don't know," he said, barely getting the words out of his constricted throat.

"I bet you don't." I brought my fist over his left ear, bringing it down like a jack hammer. The sonofabitch was bigger than I was and I didn't know where all this nerve was coming from. But it was coming.

"Who're you working for, motherfucker?" I shook him, battering his head against the ground. His nose was bleeding badly.

"The meadows . . ." he said.

"What meadows? What the fuck are you talking about?"

"The meadows . . . the meadows by the junction."

"What junction, you bastard?" I pummeled his face with my fist. "Who're you working for?"

The man shook his head. He had guts, I had to admit. I slammed him again. The back of his skull bounced off the cement.

Then I heard a shot.

13

I SAT ON my porch listening to Bach's French Suite Number Six and watching the sun come up over the San Gabriels. Dawn could be beautiful in L.A., misty-gold the way it must have been a few hundred years ago when Father Serra first eased his fat Spanish ass down the Camino Real. But this one did nothing for me. I wasn't in the mood.

I reached for the thermos and poured some coffee. I hadn't slept all night, replaying the events at Mt. Olympus in my mind, and my thoughts were getting murkier by the minute. What happened? I wasn't sure. It was difficult to see clearly, as if everything were deliberately obscured or performed symbolically like the Dumb Show in an Elizabethan Tragedy.

I thought it through again.

I heard the shot.

I jumped to my feet and turned in the direction of the French Provincial facade. The door was still open. I took a step toward it. The bastard at my feet lunged at me, but I kicked him in the face, sending him back into the fender of his car. He wasn't moving anymore. Then I ran through the door in a crouch to the end of the building site.

At first I couldn't see anything but the lights of Hollywood. The Capitol Records building was down to my left near where the freeway cut a diagonal through Sunset and across Melrose and Santa Monica. On the next ridge, there was a statue of Hermes illuminated by a green spotlight. Two men were outlined against it. One of them was backing away with his hands up. The other, the man with the Saturday Night Special, advanced on him with his gun in his hand. They weren't more than fifteen feet apart. I came closer.

"Jonas, don't do it . . . please." I thought I heard Sebastian say. His voice trembled.

"No chance, punk. You've had it!"

I started in, but before I could move, the man fired again. It looked like point-blank range but the shot missed, the bullet careening into the first of a row of mock-Corinthian columns, shattering the fluting.

"Wine!" Sebastian shouted, throwing himself on the ground and crawling behind the column.

I yelled and ran down the side of the hill. The one with the gun turned and headed toward me. I circled around a hedge and continued up the other side in back of Sebastian. The hood gripped his pistol with both hands and trained it on me.

"Move it, Sebastian. Go!" I shouted.

The county coordinator stood and started running, but tripped over a rock at the edge of the driveway. The gunman came up behind him, aiming at his back. He fired, the bullet dispersing the gravel ten feet away. The bastard must have been the worst shot in Nevada.

"Hey, Wyatt Earp!" I called out. "I've got a gun too."

The hood wheeled around in my direction. I held my fist under my jacket, jabbing a thumb through the denim. He stared at me for a moment. Sebastian clambered to his feet and began running again, out toward the main road.

"Bullshit, buddy! All you got in there is your pudgy little fist."

He lifted his gun to eye level. But I didn't wait to see if his marksmanship would improve. I ran after Sebastian like a gazelle. Seconds later he started firing. The first shot landed six inches from my right toe. The second created a temporary vacuum under my left earlobe. The third was so close I didn't realize I wasn't hit until I caught up with Sebastian at the bottom, hiding among the cypresses.

"In here." I pointed to a temporary tool shack erected at the edge of the development.

We waited inside without talking. I stood at the door with a heavy shovel in my hand. Twice we heard footsteps within fifty feet of the shack. Sebastian was breathing heavily and I was sure the bastard would blast through the wall, spattering our guts over the workbench. But ten minutes passed and nothing happened. After twenty minutes I opened the door. We were at the far end of another building site. The night was dark, silent. The road winding to the top of Mt. Olympus—empty.

"What'd you find out?" Sebastian asked me as I climbed back to the car.

"Nothing much. Something about the meadows. I couldn't figure it. . . . What about this Jonas?" I let it out casually, hoping to catch him off guard.

"Jonas?" he asked. His expression betrayed nothing.

"Yeah, the sonofabitch who was taking the shots at us."

"Was that his name? How did you know?"

"That's what you called him yourself."

Sebastian started to laugh. "I called him that?"

" 'Jonas, don't do it . . . please.' "

The county coordinator shook his head. "I must have been pretty nervous. What I was saying was 'Jesus, don't do it . . . please.' What would you have said under the circumstances?"

I didn't answer. We had reached the top of the hill. His car was where we had left it, but the green Chevy was gone, leaving a trail of rubber halfway around the circle.

14

H E'S JUST A two-bit Nevada hood, the kind that would dry-gulch a blind man for $1.85."

Koontz shrugged with a certain snugness. It was mid-morning and we were sitting at the counter of Winchell's doughnut place on Glendale Boulevard. The cop had a maple bar in front of him and a cup of black coffee.

"For you I wouldn't do diddly-shit."

"What do you want, Koontz? Justice or law? If he were a peace marcher, you'd pistol-whip your own mother to find out who he was."

"The right of privacy, Wine. As you know, every citizen has the right to be protected from random snooping into his personal affairs." The policeman swallowed the maple bar in two bites and washed it down with his coffee. "What do you want him for?"

"To get to the heart of this Lila Shea business. You want it solved, don't you?"

"What's his name?"

"Jonas."

"Jonas what?"

"I don't know."

"Is it his first name or last name?"

"I don't know that either."

Koontz looked at me in disgust. "That's all you've got?" With his left hand, he signalled the waitress to bring him a cheese danish and a second cup of coffee.

"Well, it could be Jonah, not Jonas. I wasn't that close and the other party was speaking quickly."

"The other party?"

"Sorry." I smiled at him.

"Now come on, Wine. What's going on here?"

"It's very simple, Koontz." I spoke slowly, distinctly. "I want you to find out the identity of a bimbo named Jonas, or possibly Jonah. He's about five feet eleven, hair blonde, eyes blue, solid build. He probably drinks a lot because of the redness in his cheeks. He carries a Saturday Night Special and goes around with a buddy who drives a green 1971 Chevelle with phony Nevada license plates."

"Uhuh . . . and how am I going to do that?"

"The wheels of justice, pal. You've got the materials— computers, files. This bird must have spent twelve of the last fifteen years in the slam." I wrote the details of his identity on a paper napkin and passed them to him.

"And what if I do? What's in it for me?"

"Nothing."

"Nothing?"

"Glory, Koontz. The glory of a solved case. You'll be hell's own bloodhound. And just think. I'm bringing you the first solid clue you've got."

"Our first solid clue was your fingerprints on Lila Shea's dashboard. You're about a quarter of an inch from arrest, Wine."

The waitress came over with the cheese danish. Koontz sliced it in half, eating it as rapidly as the maple bar. When he had finished, the waitress reached under the counter and presented him with a box of a dozen doughnuts, neatly tie with a ribbon. It had his name on it. Eugene Koontz.

"You know we private citizens pay for that stuff," said, standing and pointing to the box. "I bet you're the type who sleeps on the beat too." I crossed toward the door. "Oh, by the way, you'd better look into this fast. I heard rumor about a freeway explosion the morning of May 31. Of course that might just be a rumor."

Koontz muttered into his coffee as I left the restaurant.

I headed across Glendale Boulevard and up the hill on Alvarado opposite the radio antennae. I wanted to find out Alora Vazquez had returned from the *campo*. There were some questions I wanted to ask her, a matter of a purchase had made at Thriftymart earlier that morning. But I decided to stop home first and call a friend who was a public defender in Las Vegas. When I got to the door, the phone was ringing again. This time I was able to reach it before stopped, but I hesitated, sure it was Koontz eager to pun me about the freeway explosion. I let it ring a few more times, enjoying the image of the rumpled cop stewing in the phone booth next to Winchell's, before I picked it up. But the voice on the other end bore about as much resemblance to Koontz's as Judith Anderson reciting Seneca in Latin.

"Good morning, Mr. Wine. This is Oscar Procari speaking."

"Senior or Junior?"

"Senior . . . I hope I didn't call at a bad time."

"Not at all, Mr. Procari. I'm glad you did."

"Because I would like to invite you out to my house for a talk. I think we have a great deal to say to each other."

"When would you like me to come?"

"Right now." His voice was flat and uncomplicated like someone used to giving orders without having them contradicted. He continued before I could formulate a response. "My address is 102 Bermuda Lane, Rolling Hills."

"I'm on my way."

I hung up.

Traffic was light around the interchange and in ten minutes I was on the Harbor Freeway heading south. I sped by Century Boulevard and Watts and the Cal State campus behind the oil refineries in Dominguez Hills. In a few minutes I could see the San Pedro docks and the bridge to Terminal Island. I turned off and cut over to Elvira Boulevard and then up the Coast Highway to Palos Verdes. The Marineland spire loomed in front of me where a series of cliffs dropped sharply into the ocean. A group of scuba divers were reclaiming garbage off the point. I continued around the bend and turned up into the hills on Amalfi Way.

I had visited Rolling Hills several years ago with Suzanne, but we didn't stay long. It's not the kind of place you'd call hospitable. The intention is quite the opposite—to exclude the outside world, not in the coarse, planned manner of the new developments with their movie studio guard houses and electronic surveillance gadgets, but through shame. How could you break a stained glass window just to make off with a paltry color TV? Or defile their lovely tree-lined streets with a poorly-maintained 1947 Buick?

Bermuda Lane was on the other side of the hill in a wooded gully out of direct sight of the ocean. A trio of teen-age girls on horseback dressed in English riding costumes cantered past me as I turned into the driveway of number 102. The driveway was gravel and ran for perhaps fifty yards, surrounded on both sides by rows of green juniper cut low in the bonsai style. I drove down it to Procari's house, an enlarged California bungalow similar to hundreds that lined the older areas of Los Angeles. But this one was perfect. Every shingle, every wooden beam appeared to have been crafted by hand. I guessed it had been built by Greene and Greene, famous architects of the 1920's.

I parked by the sun porch next to a Mercedes limousine and a Land Rover. When I arrived at the front door, a lanky young woman was standing there in a bikini. Her skin was well browned from the sun. She was peeling at the crest of her forehead near where a pair of tinted glasses were pushed back into her auburn hair, cut short in the European manner.

"You must be here for Oscar," she said without smiling. The accent was Scandinavian. She turned and walked off into the house, knowing I was watching her slim buttocks undulate in the flesh-colored suit.

I took a step forward into the foyer, but before I could adjust my eyes to the light and get a look around, Procari emerged from a side corridor. He was also in his bathing suit with a towel draped over his neck, a short, stocky man, about five foot seven, but hard and vigorous. He must have been in his sixties. His silver hair was combed straight back over his head with the sideburns clipped modishly at his lower earlobe. On the fourth finger of his right hand, he wore a heavy gold ring with a large blue stone.

"Mr. Wine," he said, extending that hand. "I'm sorry to bring you out here on such short notice but I've a 5:00 flight to catch. I wanted to talk with you before I left."

"Happy to be here," I said, following him into the living room. It was over seventy feet long with dark mahogany panelling and antique Navajo blankets hanging from wrought iron hooks. Through the window I could see the young Scandinavian woman walking across the grass toward the pool.

"I understand you're looking for my son," he said, sliding his feet into a pair of house slippers.

"Who told you that?"

He didn't answer but continued through the living room

and into the study. It was masculine and leathery, lined with elaborate archery equipment and photographs of Procari hunting doves in the desert. A baccarat table stood against the wall next to an ebony roulette wheel. Procari pulled a chair from behind his desk, indicating for me to sit down.

"What have you found out about him, Mr. Wine?"

"Nothing much. I'm not really looking for your son, Mr. Procari. I was under the impression he died in an automobile accident two years ago."

"You mean he killed himself."

"I didn't know that."

"Well, he did."

"Why?"

"To get back at me. Ever since he was a little boy he had been trying to get back at me." He walked around the other side of the desk and sat in a swivel chair. "You needn't look so puzzled, Mr. Wine. It's quite basic. The son rises up to destroy the father. Oedipus and Laius. . . . May I get you something to drink?"

Procari pressed a buzzer and a squat Indian woman appeared as if out of the blankets and stood by my chair with a distant expression on her face.

"Gin and tonic."

"The same, Maria."

She departed through a swinging door.

"You're certain it was suicide then?"

"As certain as this." He stared at me for a moment, then swung around in his chair to pull a window cord. The curtain drew back revealing a wide window vista of the ocean. The Coast Highway was surprisingly close. In the water, the shoreline bent out to a promontory where a strong surf beat against the rocks, sending spray onto the road above. It was Deadman's Curve. Procari noticed my look of recognition. "You don't have 'accidents' in full view of your father's study, do you, Mr. Wine?"

We sat there without talking. I watched the waves smash into the shore. A young boy was walking his dog along the side of the road. Soon Maria returned with the glasses, two Schweppes bottles, a bottle of Booth's, lime and ice. Procari mixed the drinks himself in front of me, slicing the lime with some skill.

"I see you're a Yale man," I said, pointing to the heavy gold ring with the blue stone.

"Class of '30." He stirred my drink and passed it over. "The first American of Italian extraction admitted to Skull and Bones, I believe. . . . How's the drink?"

"You know there's been one thing I don't understand, Mr. Procari. If you're so certain your son is dead, how come you wanted to talk to me?"

Procari looked down at his desk. "I don't know. I don't know myself. I suppose I keep hoping. . . . I feel pretty guilty about this, as you might imagine." He paused for a moment, waiting for that to sink in. "So if there is a possibility, if anybody finds my boy . . . finds Oscarino . . . I want it to be me. It has to be me. If it were someone else, I couldn't live with myself. That's why I want to hire you, Mr. Wine. As an insurance policy against my own failure."

"Hire me?"

"Yes."

"I'm working for somebody, now, Mr. Procari."

"I know. I won't ask you who it is—or what it's about. I'll offer you twice what they're paying and ten thousand dollars at the end, if you find him." Procari fidgeted. "You don't know how painful this is to me, Mr. Wine."

"Why me, Procari?"

"Look, what's your price? Whatever it is, I'll pay it. It's worth it to have Oscarino back."

"Let's get this straight. I couldn't even consider working for you until I know who put you on to me."

Procari looked up, a thought flickering in his brain and

then disappearing. He took a sip of his gin and tonic. "Isabel La Fontana," he said.

"Isabel La Fontana? Don't tell me you're involved with Satanism too?"

Procari waved me off with a wry smile. "There were other reasons to know La Fontana in the old days."

I looked through the side window toward the pool. The Scandinavian had taken off her bikini and was bouncing on the high board. Her firm breasts moved with the bounce. Then she kicked her legs in and snapped them back in a perfect swan dive, her lovely body rippling through the water. It was clear Procari knew what he was talking about.

"Is there anything I should know about your son? Anything you haven't told me?"

"I don't think so."

"Nothing?"

"It was always the same. I gave him everything and he threw it back in disgust. Boats, cars, businesses. Even Skull and Bones. At great personal sacrifice I made sure he was chosen. But on Tap Night, when the old members came around, he left a dead rat on his pillow in a pool of blood with a note telling them he would never accept anything won for him by his father. Maybe he had a point, Mr. Wine."

"Maybe."

"Do you think he could still be alive?"

"Possibly. People disappear and come back again. A new identity is simple and all you need for plastic surgery is the money."

"And you think you can find him?"

"I can't promise anything, Mr. Procari."

"But you will work for me?"

"I can't even promise that."

He seemed perturbed. I peered around him at the baccarat table where a newspaper was spread-eagled on the green felt under a stack of magazines. The headline read:

"DILLWORTHY ACCUSES OPPONENT OF . . ." The rest was obscured by the March *Harper's*. Part of the article below was circled in red with some numbers.

Procari leaned in and held me by the forearm. His grip was strong. "Mr. Wine. You must understand. This is not a small matter to me. . . . Do you have children of your own?"

"Two boys."

"Then put yourself in my place. Think how it would be if they were grown up, in their thirties, and one of them killed himself because of you. Think of that. Then you will understand my pain."

Procari released his grip. The Scandinavian woman entered the back door, her hair still wet from the pool. She stood there for a moment, looking at us. Then she bent over the roulette wheel to implant a kiss on Procari's brow.

15

I LEFT PROCARI'S place a few minutes later with the promise I would think over his offer. Driving down Bermuda Lane, I stopped for a moment to admire a jacaranda tree. It was late spring and the lavender flowers were in full bloom. A cascade of bougainvillaea flowed over the wall behind it. Sitting there, I considered going back on foot and having another look at the financier's house, but decided against it. A man like that would have his grounds pretty closely guarded and if there was anything worth seeing, it was probably inside.

I proceeded down the hill to the Coast Highway and onto the Harbor Freeway. Traffic was heavier now and continued to mount as I approached the Civic Center where the Hollywood and San Bernardino Freeways intersect with the Harbor, the famous Interchange pictured in so many aerial photographs of Los Angeles. I wondered if this was the spot Eppis had selected for his detonation. It would be the logical choice to guarantee nationwide publicity. I drove past, turning off the freeway on Second Street and following the ramp behind the Music Center over to Sunset. Soon I was in East Los Angeles again. It didn't take me long to find Alora Vazquez' apartment the second time. Just as before, I parked in front of the synagogue and got out, carrying the slim package from Thriftymart under my arm.

I headed to the back of the court and knocked on her door. No one answered. I knocked again. Still nothing. After a moment's hesitation, I walked down to the side window. The bed was unmade and a half-finished glass of orange juice stood on the end table, but the lights were out and the apartment empty. There was a sense of hasty departure. Something ominous. Looking down, I noticed the window had been smashed just above the flower box and then sealed off with a piece of plywood. The screen itself had been ripped along the edge as if the apartment had been broken into. I continued around to the rear and knocked on the back door. Then I twisted the handle, trying to force it open. The lock began to give.

"Looking for something?"

The voice came from behind me. I spun around, shielding my face with my arms.

Two men were standing there.

I studied them through my fingers. It was the guy from the Studebaker and a buddy of his who looked like a promising light-heavy. The brother held his knife in his hand and was picking at a poinsettia branch to the right of my rib cage.

"Hello," I said, pulling down my arms and putting on my most winning smile. "Remember me?"

"What do you want?"

"I . . . uh . . . was just looking for your sister."

"My sister isn't home."

"Yeah . . . well, do you know where she is?"

The brother didn't answer. With a flick of the wrist, he sliced the branch from the tree, letting it fall to the ground at my feet.

The buddy stepped forward.

Another friend in a denim work shirt and Pancho Villa moustache appeared at the door of the next apartment. Slowly he moved down into the patio.

"Look, guys, once was enough." My voice was shrill, empty. "I've got an aged grandmother and this just might push her over."

The brother stared at me. "Someone tried to kill my sister last night."

"Funny. Someone tried to kill me last night too."

"That so?"

"Maybe it was the same someone."

"Oh yeah. Who was that?"

"A couple of skinheads in a green Chevy. One of them carried a piece."

The three men looked at each other.

"She's at rehearsal," the brother said.

I sat in the back of the warehouse watching the members of the *Teatro Comunal* work out. They were a mixed group, some of them with a lot of talent and others you wouldn't want to cast in a high school production of *Charlie's Aunt*. But they were enthusiastic and listening hard to Alora who was director in the absence of her father. They were in the midst of warm-up exercises when I arrived, touching each other's faces with their eyes closed and bumping shoulders like football players. Then they put on masks and began one of their *actos*. It concerned a gang leader in the barrio who was shot by a cop and came back to haunt his friends during the investigation. Alora had them do it again and sat down next to me.

"The group hasn't been the same without my father. . . . No concentration."

"They look okay to me. I understand you had visitors last night."

"How do you know?" she snapped.

"Your brother told me."

"Jorge told you? That's none of your business!"

"I think I know who they were." I exaggerated to get a rise out of her but she didn't bite. "Any word from your father?"

She shook her head and moved away from me, heading up to the stage to deliver instructions. The actors gathered around her at the apron. "Dance it," I heard her say. "Dance the finale. Then invite the audience to join in. . . ."

I walked around to the side and leaned against the warehouse wall. It was covered with Chicano graffiti I couldn't read. After another run-through, the rehearsal was over and the actors filed out the stage exit. Alora stood alone at the apron.

"You're still here? What do you want? Are you going to play the big hero and find my father?"

"Maybe." I took the package from under my arm and removed a record album, handing it to her. "Have you ever seen this before?"

"*Voices of Dissent.*" Her voice quavered slightly as she read the jacket. The liner notes had already yellowed from the years in the Thriftymart bin. "Michael Ofari, Howard Eppis and Luis Vazquez."

She signalled for me to follow her.

Later I sat in her living room. Two copies of *Voices of Dissent* lay on the coffee table—mine and her father's—next to a couple of .38 shells Alora had dug out of her bedroom wall that morning. Outside, her brother and his friend stood guard in the patio.

"He was listening to it all the time," she said, "before he disappeared . . . as if the record were a time machine taking him back to 1968."

"What about Eppis?"

"I never knew him."

"Did your father ever have contact with him after they made the record together?"

"Not that I know of."

"Did he ever talk about him?"

She thought for a moment. "He felt sorry for him. I remember we were watching a documentary of the Chicago Convention. One of those television rehashes of the year's news. They had footage of Eppis leading a demonstration in a Mickey Mouse cap. My father said it was sad that Howard was so confused between revolution and his own self-interest, that he wanted to change society but he was more intent on calling attention to himself."

"Your father sounds pretty militant."

"Not really. He was for anything he thought would help the Chicano. He even supported Hawthorne in this campaign."

"Did he ever mention anything about Satanism?"

"Satanism?" She laughed. "No."

"What about a man called Oscar Procari, Jr.? Sometimes known as King Nestor."

"Never heard of him."

"Then why'd you follow me into that bar?"

"My father left an address in case anything happened to him."

"23 Columbia Drive?"

"Yes. . . . My brother saw you come by there the day after he disappeared. Now the building's gone."

"What about the two fifties in your purse?"

"Unemployment money."

I leaned back on the sofa next to her with my head against the bookshelf. I expected to see a political poster, but a Manet print was pinned to the wall opposite me. The bulletin board beneath it was filled with photographs of the *Teatro.* I liked her apartment. It smelled good, not of perfume and sachets, but like a real woman lived in it, a woman who worked and sweated and fucked on top of the sheets when the weather was hot.

"I'll have to ask you to leave," she said, standing and unlocking the door. "I have a meeting tonight and I want to have dinner."

I didn't move. I picked up the slugs and rolled them about in my hand like Captain Queeg. "Why don't we have it together?"

"What for?" She stared at me with her hand on the door handle.

I shrugged.

"You're going to find my father and you want me as a prize, is that it? I heard that's how private detectives operate."

"I saw that on *Mannix* once. Only it never seems to happen to me."

"Why do you suppose that is?"

"I don't know. How about something to eat? You must know some good places around here."

"All right," she said.

We drove down Soto Street to the Restaurante Merida, a hole-in-the-wall with four formica tables and an animated waterfall advertising Coors Beer. They had Yucatan-style food and Alora told me to order *panuchos* with black beans. It turned out to be a kind of Mayan tostada in a dark, pungent sauce. The taste of the beans was more delicate than the usual frijoles. Alora talked about her family. She was born in the Yucatan, near the Island of Cozumel, where her father worked on a coffee plantation. When she was six, her mother died and her father brought the family up to the States, first to the El Paso area and then to the San Joaquin Valley and then to Los Angeles. It was in the San Joaquin Valley, near Delano, that they had become involved with Chicano theater. A group had been formed there, splintering off from the *Teatro Campesino* and Luis Vazquez had been chosen to lead it. He didn't know much about acting, but he learned fast and so did Alora and Jorge, her brother, although he didn't like it much. He liked to fix cars. After the group was really together, they moved down to Los Angeles to help organize in the Barrio.

We drank a few beers and then sat there awhile over our coffee. I was feeling pretty mellow, looking at Alora and watching the Coors waterfall splash over a smiling fisherman. I didn't like the idea of returning to an empty house with nothing but Clue and hash to keep me company. But the waiter came with the bill and we left. Driving back to her place, Alora sat closer to the driver's side of the Buick. My hand fell on her shoulder at a stoplight and I let it stay there. She didn't move away. A sad Cuban *canción* drifted over from the jukebox of a local bar.

"Do you think my father's alive?" she asked, turning toward me, our thighs touching.

"I don't know," I said. "I don't know."

When we got back to the apartment, her brother and his buddy were still there, tossing the knife into the trunk of an avocado tree. I allowed the car to idle, trying to figure a way to go in with her, but the men weren't leaving.

The brother turned toward us.

"The meeting's started," he said.

Alora nodded. She jumped out of the car and crossed the patio without looking back.

I stared after her for a moment then drove off into the night. I didn't know where I was headed. The car appeared to be guiding itself, flat out on the Golden State Freeway. The road was filled with eight-wheel trucks bound for Bakersfield and diesel tankers spewing black exhaust as they carried the oil from Long Beach to San Francisco and points north. I curved around Griffith Park and detoured onto the Ventura where the freeways intersect in Burbank. Soon I was northbound through the San Fernando Valley, speeding around the other side of the park past Warner Drive. Universal Studios loomed up in the distance followed by the off-ramp to Laurel Canyon.

I pulled up behind Madas' Jaguar. All the lights were out except for a flickering from the boys' bedroom and an orange glow from Suzanne's. I got out of the car, closing the door quietly, and walked over to the house I had bought almost a year ago but slept in for only two weeks. Jacob was sitting up in bed watching a cowboy movie on TV with Simon asleep beside him. In the next room, a candle glowed behind a cellophane screen, reflecting the naked backs of Madas and Suzanne. His legs were crossed in the lotus and she was seated on top of him, in the opposite direction, straddling his torso with her toes pointed forward. They both had their eyes closed. I wondered if this was one of those Tibetan positions I had read about, the ones in which Tantric priests were able to hold an erection for six hours. I stood there for a moment, watching them frozen in a sexual trance. Had I expected her to be alone?

When I got home, I had a smoke and crawled into bed. I lay on my back stroking my penis, thinking about Lila Shea in the old Berkeley days, about us making it on mescaline in a eucalyptus grove in Tilden Park. But it didn't work. A vision of Suzanne and Madas kept floating into my mind, spoiling it; the kids in the next room stupefied in front of the television set. . . . But then I conjured up Alora, naked on the beaches of the Yucatan, a jungle orchid tucked in her ear, bending over me, and things felt a little better for a while.

16

N O FINGERPRINTS!" SAID the clerk, his voice squeaking peremptorily. He towered over me, standing on a stool behind the counter at the county coroner's office, the lower half of his jaw wrinkled in a prune-like sneer.

"Why's that?"

"Do I have to say why? There just aren't any."

"What about x-rays?"

"We don't have them."

"What do you mean you don't have them?"

"Do you expect us to keep x-rays on every case that comes through here?" He waved his finger at me like a schoolmarm chastising the class dunce. "This inquest was over two years ago. And even if we did have them, you wouldn't be allowed to see them anyway."

"They were cited in the newspaper reports."

"Indeed." The coroner's clerk snorted, stepping down from his stool and pushing the file to the other side of the counter. From the front he looked like one of those ads for cut-rate clothes on the Late Show—a complete wardrobe for $89.95. He was all color-coordinated in a lime green shirt with forest pants and a yellow tie; but chintzy, as if he would unravel the moment you pulled one thread from the seat of his trousers. "And now, if you'll excuse me, you're taking up county time."

"Is that so?" I said, edging down the counter to the file. "May I have a look at this?"

"Absolutely not. It's against county rules."

"County rules? But it's already ten o'clock."

I pointed up at the wall behind him. The clerk looked puzzled. He turned around in the direction I was pointing. When he had his back fully to me, I reached over his shoulder and grabbed hard on his sweet yellow tie, yanking it backwards. He sputtered and choked.

"One move and you'll have an Adam's apple up your nose!"

"Hey!" he shouted.

I twisted the tie a quarter turn to the left, shutting him up, and reached down for the file with my other hand.

"Sorry to violate county rules," I said, flipping the file open in front of me. "I've always had a deep feeling of respect for the Board of Supervisors."

I looked down at the coroner's report, skimming the information for something that might prove useful to me. Procari had lived in the Sunset Hills, not far from Isabel La Fontana, and was thirty-one years old at the time of death. He was five foot ten inches in height, brown hair, brown eyes, with a long scar on his right thigh from a childhood injury. There was a photograph of him in his Satan regalia looking like something out of an old Conrad Veidt movie. The next page had a silhouette drawing of the remains with an explanation by the examining physician. The bones themselves had been badly charred as if the body itself had been completely incinerated before the vehicle ever struck the water—a most remarkable case, according to the physician. A forensic surgeon, Dr. Adrian Wincorn, had been called in for consultation. Dr. Wincorn said the car must have exploded at least two hundred yards from the curve in order to have caused such severe burns. A faulty fuel line in the Maserati's delicate intestines, perhaps. The inner organs of beast and fowl. Or a deliberate suicide, if one were to believe the father.

"Unnnnh!" The clerk tried to scream for help.

"Shut up."

A signature at the bottom of the page indicated the bones had been removed to Dr. Wincorn's laboratory for further study, but the space set aside to be stamped on their return was unmarked.

"Now how do you explain an oversight like that?" I asked the clerk without giving him a chance to answer. "Isn't that against the county rules? Not on the take, are you?" I released the tie and he fell back into the xerox machine. "I'd hate to think our public officials were on the take. That's not the kind of thing that inspires people's confidence."

I checked the address under Wincorn's name—147 N. Cranberry Drive, Beverly Hills—and tossed the file on the desk in front of him.

147 N. Cranberry was the typical Beverly Hills "Doctor's Building"—a glass cube over five layers of subterranean parking with elevators that worked by thermal contact and pastel drawings of Paris on the wall. It had an overpriced pharmacy in the lobby and a receptionist with an eye for social class equal to the maitre d' of the best restaurant in town. I eased past her and consulted the black-felt office listings. Dr. Wincorn's name was nowhere to be found. I walked back to the receptionist.

"Didn't a Dr. Adrian Wincorn have his offices here?" I asked.

"Dr. Wincorn is no longer with us."

"Why not?"

"Dr. Wincorn is not the kind of doctor who fits in at 147 North Cranberry."

"I see. Well where is Dr. Wincorn then?"

"I shouldn't know."

She turned away from me to deal with a matron in a macrame stole. Shouldn't know, my ass. I walked around her into the pharmacy, stopping a young black salesgirl smiling behind an ad for Preparation H.

"Have you been working here long?"

"Three years."

"Remember a Dr. Wincorn?"

"Wincorn ... Wincorn ..." She picked up a bottle of Noxzema and replaced it on the shelf. "Stay away from him. A regular butcher."

"I wasn't planning on seeing him for an illness."

"How about your girlfriend?"

"Where can I find him?"

"A malpractice suit, huh? He's at the Self-Determination Clinic, if they haven't condemned the place yet."

"Where's that?"

"Over by the airport."

Over by the airport was right. I found the Self-Determination Clinic on a little street behind Century Boulevard about twenty yards off the New York flight line. It was tucked between a hangar and a car rental agency. A low-flying 747 rattled the window panes as I approached the front steps. The roar was deafening. I walked around to the side of the building examining the facade. The shades were drawn and decorated in pink with rainbow decals. A sign on the back door was ringed with flowers and read "Patients Entrance Only." While I stood there, a Dodge van pulled up driven by a heavyset man in a cowboy hat and dark glasses. A nurse got out, followed by two young girls who looked around sixteen. They looked scared and carried overnight bags, one plaid and one grey. The girl with the grey bag had been crying. She had a sticker on her purse which said "Tulsa High Boosters '72" with an oil well in the background.

"Is it all right?" she asked.

"I don't know, Miss Henderson. Money order or certified check only." The nurse shook her head and stepped back a few paces to speak with the driver. "Jane Ellen Larkin. United Flight No. 31 from Salt Lake."

He nodded and drove off.

The nurse turned toward me.

"May I help you?"

"I'd like to speak with Dr. Wincorn. I'm from the coroner's office."

The nurse blushed.

Five minutes later I was sitting in Wincorn's office. The doctor was about to explain himself when another 747 roared overhead making speech impossible.

"Listen," he said when it had passed. "I don't know what this is about but this is a legitimate business. Abortion is legal in the state of California when authorized by two physicians—or haven't you heard?" He pointed at the clinic license over his head.

"I'm not here to question your right to perform abortions, doctor."

Through his office window, I could see the van already pulling back into the clinic lot and depositing the new patient. Fast work indeed. A young girl in a pastel rain coat stepped into the van and headed off for the airport.

"Our prices are fair. $175 for a vacuum, $285 for a D&C. That includes picking the girls up at the plane and returning them the same day so their friends back in Iowa don't know a thing."

"I told you I'm not interested in abortions."

"Then what do you want?" Wincorn addressed me flatly, with an undertone of implied threat. He was a powerful man with the trim body of a twenty-three-year-old, but the wrinkled face of someone much older, in his forties. A Jack LaLanne or a Vic Tanney. He must have spent a lot of time working out.

"I'm interested in the Procari case."

"The what?"

"The Procari case."

"I don't know what you're talking about."

"Come on, doctor. Think back. It was only two years ago." Wincorn shook his head. Another plane flew past and I waited to continue. "A thirty-one-year-old man shot over Deadman's Curve in a Maserati. You know about it. Your name's on the coroner's report."

"It is?"

"You signed out with the evidence and never brought it back."

"What evidence?"

"Some bones supposedly belonging to the victim. The only question is which one. They must have belonged to some victim or other. Unless they were animal bones."

"I don't have the faintest idea what this is all about."

"You don't? Look, Wincorn, you've got a lucrative thing going here. You must be doing more business than Planned Parenthood and the La Leche League combined."

"Well?"

"You wouldn't want to upset it over some little oversight in a coroner's report, some little miscue which you and I know was just a tiny accident in an otherwise impeccable career."

"Listen, buddy, I don't even think you're with the coroner's office, but whoever—"

"Whoever I am I can still inform the proper authorities."

Wincorn sat back in his chair. "Yeah."

"But I can assure you, doctor, I haven't the slightest interest in you. If you've spent the last ten years giving physical therapy to ax murderers, that's your affair. All I want is some information."

"What?"

"Just tell me what you know about the Procari death and I'll leave you alone. Otherwise you can kiss the Self-Determination Clinic good-bye along with your own license to practice medicine in the state of California."

The nurse stuck her head in the door. "You're wanted in surgery, doctor."

"What happened to those bones, Wincorn?"

"Tell them to wait," he told the nurse. She ducked out, shutting the door behind her. The doctor was sweating profusely.

"I don't know. I never saw them."

"What do you mean you never saw them?"

"They were handed to me in a black box at the coroner's office and I delivered it to a man at the Enco Station on Sunset and Alvarado. I never even looked inside."

"Who? Who was the man?"

"I never saw him again. He gave me five thousand dollars and disappeared."

"Who was he, Wincorn?"

"A man in a Dacron suit, slate grey."

"What was his name?"

The doctor reached into his desk and pulled out a sterile gauze pad, breaking it open to mop his brow. Sweat was soaking through the collar of his white coat.

"If I tell you, they'll kill me."

"If you don't tell me, there'll be a lot of cheap abortion equipment up for auction. What's the name, Wincorn? You can trust me."

"Jonas," he said. "Phil Jonas."

17

W E WANT HAWTHORNE! We want Hawthorne! We want Hawthorne! We want Hawthorne!" Klieg lights over Wilshire Boulevard. Traffic stacked up along the Miracle Mile. Television cameras. Scaffolding. Dignitaries. Crowds. The fetid stench of bigtime politics.

I stood in the entryway of a garage opposite Hawthorne Headquarters where Sugars had told me to wait. Not to leave under any circumstances. He was busy now, but he wanted to talk with me. Definitely. After they had seen the Candidate. . . .

I leaned against the wall and watched the show. A well-scrubbed black group called the Incredibles was singing about Hawthorne as if he were God descended from the machine. They wore cardigan sweaters emblazoned with the Democratic donkey and red, white and blue straw hats perched on their discreet naturals. An Oriental girl in a miniskirt danced a restrained go-go in front of them just below a trio of Secret Service agents surveying the scene from the headquarters roof. The crowd was large, stretching down Wilshire as far as Commonwealth Avenue and around the corner to Sixth. It seemed like everybody and his brother were backing Hawthorne that night.

The group sang a soul version of "This Land Is Your Land" and the candidate emerged, flanked by his wife, a city councilman and a local black football star. It was the first time I had seen Hawthorne in the flesh, and I studied him carefully. He seemed diffident for such a rabble rouser. Under normal conditions he would have been about as charismatic as my Uncle Sid, a retired insurance agent in Larchmont, New York; but something about all the attention he was getting, the television and the lights, had elevated this mundane-looking man into a superstar. It was as if, for the moment, the dull and the bland had become the sine qua non of personal appearance. The football star standing next to him looked gauche, almost childish, in his long sideburns and velour sports jacket.

The group finished the song and a fanfare was played. As the candidate stepped to the microphone, Sugars rushed to my side. The whiz kid was livid, muttering and smashing his fist into his palm.

"Follow me," he said.

We walked through the garage to the service elevator and up to the second floor, continuing down a corridor to the main office area. The rooms were empty. Everyone had gone down to hear the candidate. Cigarettes were still burning in ashtrays. Papers were strewn over the tables with pencils and crayons on top of them. Everything left midway.

At the far end Sugars took out a set of keys and unlocked an office door, swinging it open for me. Unlike the other rooms, it was completely empty as if swept clean with a heavy-duty vacuum.

"Vanished," he said.

"Since when?"

"Since yesterday." Sugars pulled open the desk drawers. They were empty. The bulletin board was stripped. "Nothing.

Cleaned out. We tried his house, everywhere. No one can locate him. . . . Why didn't you tell me about this earlier?"

"Because I wasn't sure."

"He's a spy for Dillworthy, isn't he?"

"I don't know."

"You don't know?! Jesus."

I turned to look through the window. The view from this office provided a superb view of the candidate, halfway between the window and the street. It seemed as if we could reach out and touch his shoulder. Hawthorne was raising his hands to quiet the cheers of his supporters, but they wouldn't let him. The chorus began again: "We want Hawthorne! We want Hawthorne!" alternating with "Peace Now! Peace Now!" Sugars tugged at my sleeve.

"Can you find him?"

"I'm not sure."

"What do you mean, you're not sure? That's your business, isn't it? Being a detective and finding people?"

"I thought it was your business to screen people for important positions in this campaign. I don't know how he got to be L.A. County Coordinator in the first place."

"There's a lot of work to do. You can't check everything."

"That doesn't tell me much."

The whiz kid shrugged. "Nine months ago he walked into our Hollywood office. Hawthorne was nobody then. We needed all the aid we could get. And he worked like a demon. Day and night."

"Who'd he say he was?"

"An ex-social worker from Springfield, Missouri. Got sick of the Midwest and came out here to help the campaign. We checked that out. There's a Sam Sebastian from Springfield."

"Was."

"Was?"

"An old con game. The simplest way to take on a new identity. Find out about someone who recently died with your basic description—hair, eyes, height, age. Get a photocopy of his birth certificate from his hometown. Get a job with that and then get a social security card and anything else you need."

Sugars stroked his fat cheeks. "If he's not Sebastian, who is he?"

"He could be a man named Oscar Procari, Jr. At least it looks that way."

"Who's that?"

"A Satanist who flunked out of Yale in his senior year."

"A what? . . . I thought you were looking for Howard Eppis."

"Of course, I'm not positive. But if he's not Procari he must be connected with him somehow."

"And what about the smear? Is that for real?"

"It could be. According to a letter Sebastian—or Procari—showed me, Eppis is going to blow up a freeway on May 31 to show his undying love for Senator Hawthorne."

"That's the day after tomorrow."

I nodded.

"Jesus H. Christ!" Sugars slumped into the padded desk chair. "I didn't know he was planning to blow a freeway." He stuck one of his fancy cigars in his mouth and tried to light it, but his lighter wouldn't work. "Shit! . . . I don't understand this. How come Sebastian showed you the letter? Why would he do something like that if he's involved with the plot?"

"I don't know."

"Do you think we should call the police?"

"That's up to you."

"Jesus." He tried to light the cigar again, then tossed it in the wastebasket in disgust. In the reflection of a fluorescent bulb he looked young. Very young. Nineteen years old.

Behind him, Hawthorne had begun a speech about welfare reform, his voice penetrating the window glass. The talk wasn't generating much enthusiasm although his proposals were sound. Sugars opened and closed a drawer, then spoke again. "We could call them . . . we could call the police, but one way or the other the story would leak. Radical saboteurs in Hawthorne's campaign. Think what the press would do with that. And that's assuming the police could stop them from acting in the first place." He stood up and marched over to the wastebasket, picking out a piece of scrap paper. It was blank. "The candidate's credibility would be ruined. It'd be all over, unless . . . unless we could pin it all on Dill-worthy." The whiz kid smiled at having come up with a possible solution but my frown discouraged him. "What do you think we should do?" he asked, his voice suddenly weak and childlike. I felt uneasy in this position of power, uneasy to be part of the fate of a man as important as Hawthorne, whatever I thought of him.

I looked over at him. From the back the candidate's gestures were awkward. His movements appeared forced, as if copied at the mirror from a book of rhetoric. He accented passages of his speech with the programmed emphasis of a high school debater.

"What can we do?" Sugars repeated, but I put a finger to my lips. Someone was walking through the front room. The footsteps approached Sebastian's office. A man in a bulging overcoat appeared at the door. He pulled out a Smith & Wesson, training it on us with one straight arm and simultaneously reaching for his wallet with his other hand.

"Secret Service. What're you guys doing here?"

"Hey, put that thing away!" said Sugars. "We're with the campaign."

The agent looked suspicious. "Oh yeah. Let's see some identification." He went up and down, frisking us for weapons. Then he walked over to the window. "You realize from this angle you could assassinate the candidate with a pea shooter." He pointed his gun at the back of Hawthorne's neck and for a moment it looked as if he might do it himself.

Sugars threw his identification on the desk. "Nate Sugars. Director of Public Opinion. Hawthorne-for-President." The Secret Service man leaned over, examining Sugars' photograph on the card.

"Who's he?" he asked, nodding toward me.

"He's all right," said Sugars. "He's working with me."

The agent grunted and headed for the door. "Stay away from the window."

18

J ONAS," I SAID. "Phil Jonas."
It was close to twelve and I was standing in a
phone booth opposite Ralph's Market on the corner of
Vermont and Third.

"Doesn't ring a bell. . . . Why'd you have to call me at
this time of night, Moses?"

"Because there isn't any time. Think: Jonas. Phil Jonas."

"I'm thinking."

I drummed my fingers on the booth wall.

". . . but I'm not coming up with much."

"I thought you knew every hood in Nevada."

"Look, Moses, I'll call you tomorrow. Let me have the
morning to search this thing out."

"I'll give you an hour, Katz. Call me back at my home.
957-0745."

I hung up and drove home.

Sitting on the edge of my bed, I listened to the *Voices
of Dissent*, first Luis Vazquez and then Howard Eppis. Then
over again. Vazquez spoke quietly of the life of the migrant
worker camps and the birth of his theater, the first tour to
Tierra Amarilla and to San Jose for La Fiesta de las Rosas.

He seemed like a good man but distant, unreachable on the one-to-one level, like many authentic revolutionaries. A mass movement was more important than a personal inter-change.

But it was Eppis' voice that fascinated me. His pitch appeared to have changed in the last four years, to have lowered. The intonation was the same, almost identical, but his voice was an octave deeper—or at least a fifth. Maybe it had only been the telephone. The poor fidelity had done something to his voice. Or perhaps Earl had altered it, back then, for some reason that wasn't entirely clear to me.

I listened again.

Howard's speech was becoming maudlin. The content was thin and there was nothing very shocking about a lot of four-letter words. Not even back in 1968. It sounded as if he had constructed his remarks for no other purpose than to irritate his grandmother. But the voice was different. Shrill and excited, a cross between Smokey Robinson and Leon Trotsky with a touch of Eddie Cantor thrown in.

The phone rang and I took the record off. It was Marty Katz, my friend at the Vegas public defender's office.

"You really put me on the Nevada shit list, I want you to know."

"Sorry."

"This may be an all-night town but you can't call around everywhere at one in the morning without causing more coitus interruptus than the last two Popes combined."

"A shame," I said.

"Damn right it is. Now what'd you say the name of that joker you wanted was?"

"Jonas, Phil Jonas."

"Yeah, that's right."

A long silence. "Come on, what about it?" I said.

"There are two hoods named Phil Jonas in this state. One of them's in gambling and prostitution and the other one's in prostitution and gambling. Also they're both blonds in their mid-thirties."

"What color eyes?"

"Jumping Jehosophat, Wine. I was waking people up right and left. Do you think I asked them for particulars? Does he have a mole on his chin? Does he have a strawberry mark on his left butt?"

"My man has blue eyes."

"Well, shiver my timbers! So does every topless dancer in Reno. Look, come down here and find out for yourself. The man to see is Alfred Craw at the Palm Casino in Tonopah."

"Tonopah?"

"That's right. Tonopah. Just don't tell them who sent you."

"All right." I started to hang up.

"Oh, and, er, Wine . . . that stuff I told you about the two Phil Jonases—it's bullshit! There's only one and I hear he's murder."

The Palm Casino in Tonopah. I remembered that pisspot town, plopped down in the middle of the state about three hundred miles due east of San Francisco in the old silver mining district, a couple of gas stations, a bar, and a Sears mail-order outlet store. It couldn't have had a population of more than two thousand although it was the main truck stop between Vegas and Reno. But then nobody lived in Nevada outside the gambling centers except for a few cowboys and some nuclear physicists. The Palm Casino in Tonopah. Nine hours' drive if I took the usual route over Barstow, maybe seven hours if I went up 395 through Lone Pine and Bishop. Quite a ways to go. A ridiculous trip, in fact.

I swilled some coffee and walked outside. It was nearly 2:00 A.M. and dark clouds had obscured the moon. The Buick was parked at the end of the driveway by Jacob's red wagon. I stood on the running board and wiped the moisture from the rear window. Then I got in and turned the ignition. The transmission growled for a while after she kicked over.

Four hours later I was at the bottom of an alkali sink driving into a desert dawn. I had already crossed the state line. Heading due east, my eyes squinted at the orange sun rising behind the piñon trees. I flipped down the visor and started up the side of a mesa, pushing the old car up to eighty. I twisted the radio dial, trying to find something decent besides farm reports and early morning sermons. For $5.95 I could get a guaranteed long-playing album of Reverend Arthur C. T. Stevens reciting selections of the Gospel accompanied by the South Utah State Pentecostal Choir. A station from Castroville, California, let on that the price of avocados was going down again to $4.87 a bushel. I turned off the radio and floored the gas pedal at the top of the mesa. Maybe I could squeeze out an extra five mph.

At exactly 8:30 I pulled into Carter's Chevron at the intersection of 6 and 266 in Tonopah. My back ached and my eyelids were coated with dust. I let myself slump down in the driver's seat for a moment before I shook myself and walked into the office. The attendant gave me an odd look as I crossed past him and took the restroom key from the hook on the wall. In the bathroom mirror I realized how strange I must look in Tonopah. My hair was too long and the red stitching on my denim collar would have been out of place at a rodeo. I slicked down my hair with a ten-cent comb and some Wildroot from the dispenser, then I walked onto the main street. There were about a dozen buildings on the block but none of them resembled a casino, so I started across the street to Thompson's Cafe for a country breakfast. The air smelled clean and fresh. Off in the distance I could see the wreck of an abandoned mine jutting out from the side of the mountain.

Thompson's Cafe was a plain stone building with a wall made of empty beer bottles cemented together in the desert manner. A silver-plated horseshoe was hammered to the door. When I went inside, a cowboy was getting some flap-jacks from a broad-shouldered Indian woman in a gingham dress. A slot machine stood in the corner next to a jukebox which was playing Ferlin Husky. I sat down at the end of the counter and ordered coffee. The woman brought it to me in a mug with a bran muffin.

"From L.A.?" she asked, studying me.

"Yeah."

"I could tell. What part you from?"

"Near downtown."

"Downtown? I used to live in Lincoln Heights. You know Lincoln Heights?"

"Uhuh."

"Thompson's been everywhere," said the cowboy. "She's from Alaska. She's been to England, too. Been to England, ain't you, Thompson?"

"That's right, Charlie."

"Married to an Englishman," the cowboy continued. He reminded me of Neal Cassady. "First time I ever heard of that," he added. "An Englishman married to an Indian woman. Kind of makes you think."

"I'm looking for a place called the Palm Casino. It doesn't seem to be on the main street."

"Oh, it's on the main street all right."

The cowboy smiled up at Thompson. One of his front teeth was missing. She reached beneath the counter and flicked on a green neon sign with the words Palm Casino written in script. It was attached to the wall above the door by a metal rod. The "P" and the "C" were formed out of palm fronds. "This is it," she said, "between nine and three in the morning. Once in a while anyway. Daytimes it's Thompson's Cafe."

"They put a sign on the front door too," said the cow-boy.

"What kind of games do they play? Craps? Blackjack?"

The cowboy laughed. "Hell, no. I ain't never seen a craps table in here ever. Did you, Thompson?"

The Indian woman shook her head.

"Thompson and me don't come around nights much. You gotta have a Rolls-Royce for that."

"Rich, are they?"

"Phew!" The cowboy tugged on his Stetson for emphasis. "Coupla dudes came down in a helicopter once. Remember that, Thompson?"

"Yup."

"Scared the shit out of Michaelson's cattle herd... 'scuse the French." The cowboy sliced his way through a piece of ham, covering it with Worcestershire sauce.

"What'd they do? Bring in their own roulette wheels? Play poker?"

"None of that stuff. They used to bet real weird things, far as I could tell. You know how rich people are." The cowboy went over to the window and took a peek at my car. "No, maybe you don't. Anyway, they'd bet on anything. You name it."

"Like what?"

"Like the Florida Little League Championship. I saw two guys bet a hundred thousand dollars on that... or remember that civil war in Africa? ... Where was it, Thompson?"

"Nigeria."

"That's right, Nigeria. They bet around a half million on who'd come out of that one on top—giving odds, of course. But like I said, me and Thompson never went around much. They didn't want us to."

"Who didn't want you to? Alfred Craw?"

"Damn right. Worst snob I ever met. Thank God we don't have to put up with them much."

"You mean they're not here?"

"Goddamn, I thought you knew. They haven't been

around here in twelve, thirteen weeks. . . . Isn't that right, Thompson?"

The Indian woman nodded. "You never know when they're comin'," she said.

"Leave Thompson five hundred dollars in cash every time they come through though." The cowboy winked at me.

I felt a depression coming on like winter fog. I sat there holding the coffee in my hand until it burned. Four hundred miles of all-night driving for this? I leaned in toward Thompson.

"Did they leave a forwarding address, any place they can be reached?"

"None."

"Well, where do they come from?"

"Search me."

"There's no way I can locate them? It's very important." She shook her head.

"What about a man named Phil Jonas?" I asked. "Tall, short blond hair. Muscular. Did he ever show up for the games?"

"Never heard of him." Thompson wrote out my check on a little green pad and handed it to me. "Anything else you want to know?"

"No," I said, "no."

I stepped out onto the main street of Tonopah. The sun had risen over the mountains and a strong midday heat was building up, creating atmospheric waves over the macadam highway. I walked along the sidewalk. The stores seemed empty, barren black caves against the white light. I began to feel dizzy. It was hard moving around in the desert without sleep. I crossed the street and continued along the other side past a Singer Sewing Machine Center and a Woolworth's. They too were empty except for a pair of salesgirls who lingered in the rear of the Woolworth's by the candy counter. The people of Tonopah were lizards who crawled under rocks in the heat of the day. I headed back toward my car, cursing Marty Katz for his faulty information and myself for being such a fool as to come out here in the first place.

When I got back to the gas station, the cowboy was standing by the pump.

"Hey, fella," he said. "I've been thinkin'. One time about a year ago, maybe a year and a half, I saw some of them gamblers riding along a dirt road like they was in a big hurry."

"A dirt road? Where were they going?"

"Don't really remember . . . I think . . . no, I can't recall."

"What kind of a car were they driving?"

"A Lincoln . . . or was it a Merc? Yeah, a Merc. A Merc or an Olds."

"Where was it?"

"About a hundred miles south of here . . . give or take."

"Give or take what?"

"Fifty miles."

"Fifty miles? There must be a lot of dirt roads in fifty miles of desert."

"Sometimes. But most of them don't go nowhere. They just wind up into the mountains ten or fifteen miles and disappear."

"Disappear? Was that the kind of road they were on?"

"Go on down 266 a piece and see for yourself."

The cowboy waited for me to respond.

"Yeah . . . thanks a lot," I said.

He tipped his hat and walked back to Thompson's Cafe.

I got into my car and drove off, forking left on 266 toward Vegas and down into a valley. What was I doing? Looking for a dirt road that someone I didn't know might have been driving a year ago to a destination that was totally unknown to me? The whole adventure was absurd.

The road curved along the mountains through groves of

joshua trees and then dipped into the low desert. The vegetation diminished and the temperature increased. It must have been well over a hundred. The mutilated carcass of a coyote sauteed on the cement apron. A trio of concrete missile cylinders loomed huge out of the earth behind it. Several dirt roads curled off into the desert, but I didn't stop. I sped past, the frame of the Buick rattling like Gabby Hayes' buckboard.

The desert was low but it kept getting lower and from the saline quality of the land I guessed I was approaching Death Valley. Soon I saw an intersection with an Arco Station and a sign pointing to Death Valley Junction; a roadside diner advertised itself as the last eating place for eighty miles. I continued on but slowed a half mile beyond it. A large placard with faded lettering was propped against a boulder on the side of the road. A smaller dirt road ran off into the desert beyond it. I studied the words on the sign— COTTONWOOD MEADOWS/SLOTS—GIRLS—DANCING/14 MILES/ "YOU CAN'T GO WRONG A THE MEADOWS!"

The meadows. Cottonwood Meadows.

I pulled over to the curb and looked out at the desert. The dirt road went off in the direction of Death Valley, out toward a crease in the Panamint Range, diving over a ridge and disappearing behind the mountains. Maybe ten miles straight and another four on the far side of the rocks. A rough trip in a four-wheel drive vehicle but sheer madness in a jalopy like mine.

I switched on the radio for the time. It was nearly twelve o'clock. In fifteen or sixteen hours Howard Eppis would detonate a freeway and with it Miles Hawthorne's chances at the presidency. And here I was trying to decide whether to go off on some godforsaken road to nowhere. What could it be way out there beyond the rocks? Did they expect anyone to negotiate fourteen miles of dirt road for some measly supper club and a few slot machines? With such a faded sign the place had probably folded up years ago.

Cottonwood Meadows. Death Valley Junction. The meadows by the junction. That's what the bastard had said up on Mt. Olympus. The meadows by the junction.

I turned onto the dirt road with a jolt which almost broke the front suspension. The car lurched forward and crashed into a cactus, pushing in the front fender and wedging the body into a mound of clay. I backed up and moved out on the road again, heading out over the desert. A fine coat of dust was rising over the hood and falling in layers on the front window like an action painting. The car was a hot box. A steady stream of sweat poured down my face, soaking my shirt and pants. Another river ran down my neck and back into the padding of the seat beneath me, vaporizing on contact, the thermal equivalent of the Arctic where the spittle freezes before it reaches the ground.

After what seemed like an hour, I came to a fork in the road marked by the shell of a wrecked Oldsmobile. A yellow arrow was painted on the trunk with the words COTTONWOOD MEADOWS, 11 MI. written beneath it. Three rotten miles, that's all I'd gone. I looked forward and backward at nothing but desert. The surface of the earth shimmered in front of me. Then, off in the distance, I noticed two dots moving toward me. I watched as they appeared to bounce in midair like jack rabbits over a prairie bush, not on the dirt road, but straight over the desert itself in a direct line from the Southwest. Now I could see two men on motorcycles. Harley-Davidsons. New and shiny, even in the dust. The drivers were dressed to match in tailored cowboy shirts, cracked leather boots and authentic Los Angeles Rams football helmets. Rich ranchers. They pulled up in front of me, revving their engines.

"Cottonwood Meadows?" I shouted to them, but they

couldn't hear over the roar of the Harleys. On closer inspection I could see they were father and son. The father wore a pair of silver motorcycle goggles. He looked at me laughing, and made a circle with the thumb and index finger of his left hand. Then he thrust his right index finger through, in and out, in a coarse gesture and said something I couldn't understand. With a nod the two men took off in the direction of the meadows. They were soon out of sight, although I did my best to keep up with them, gunning the Buick along the dirt road, listening to the carburetor bang against the inside of the hood.

Within a mile the road became graded and I was able to go faster, approaching the foothills of the Panamints, red and sculpted like Indian artifacts. The car drove through a notch, continuing down still again to sea level or below at the edge of Death Valley. Up ahead I saw a clump of trees, cottonwood and ash, growing from a small oasis above what must have been a natural spring. A cluster of ranch houses stood behind the trees beside a pond with swans floating on it. A wood wagon wheel decorated the front of a very large metal trailer. The scene was idyllic, a romance of the Old West out of a John Ford film.

I continued through an archway which said COTTONWOOD MEADOWS WELCOMES YOU, past a short desert landing strip with a Cessna and a Piper Cub at the end beneath a corrugated overhang. The two Harley-Davidsons were wedged between a jeep and an International Harvester at the back of the trailer. I pulled up behind them and got out, walking around to the front. The windows were covered with pink and orange colored lights glowing on the inside. A pair of gelatin cupids danced on either side of the door. I heard the sound of cheap Mancini music coming from a scratchy victrola. A black woman dressed like a mammy in a red bandana and gingham dress opened the front door and looked at me.

"Come on in," she said.

"The water's fine!" said the rancher who had emerged out of the darkness behind her. I could see his son with his arm around a blonde in hot pants and fishnet stockings.

I stepped up into the entry room of the trailer, a waiting room of sorts ringed with paisley cushions. A couple of men in flight outfits were seated against the wall. The mammy was showing them two of the girls, one black and one white, both tall and statuesque like Vegas showgirls, but over-the-hill, the kind that would be pushed to the back of the line on weekends.

"A little of the old in and out," said the rancher, nudging me in the ribs with his elbow and swilling booze from a silver hip flask. "Like to bring the boy down every couple of weeks," he continued. "Takes the edge off, if you know what I mean."

"You always come here?"

"Best girls in the state. Everybody knows that. And safe, too. Doctor flies in every Friday to check 'em out."

I stared out at the ranch through the tinted gelatin. The swans crisscrossed in the pond under a weeping willow tree. A large older man in a cook's hat and apron ambled over to them and threw them bread crumbs from a cookie can, calling to them with a curious grunting noise. The swans hissed back and swam over to him.

"How 'bout y'all?" said the mammy, tapping me on the shoulder. She had a brunette and a redhead with her. The brunette was in a jumpsuit with a zipper down the front open to the waist.

"I don't think I could meet the price," I said.

"Price? Hell, boy, I'll pay," said the rancher, clapping me on the back. His breath reeked of bourbon. "This is your lucky day!"

I looked more closely at the brunette. Her hips rounded off gently to a pair of slim curvy legs. She wore deep ma-

roon lipstick and dark eyelashes. Her pale, almost translu-
cent skin looked like some Berlin cabaret dancer in the
twenties. She had a soft, decadent feeling to her that was
definitely appealing.

But what was I thinking about? I had a job to do.

"Come on, boy!" The rancher clapped me on the back
again. "What're you waiting for?"

The brunette smiled. She took me by the hand and led
me down the hall past a series of cubicles and a small pro-
jection room. I didn't resist. It had been a long time. Besides,
who cared about a murder and a big election fix? They
could wait.

"What's your name?" Her room had a single plastic rose
on the bedstand and a framed Lautrec print on the wall. La
Moulin de la Galette. Patchouly incense burned from a brass
pot above the wardrobe.

"Moses," I said.

"I'm Cynthia."

She slipped out of her jumpsuit and stood by the mirror,
her body highlighted by the yellow bulb. Her breasts were
firm and sharply pointed. Then she moved toward me and
we embraced, falling onto her light folding cot. Out in the
corridor, I could hear some people laughing. She reached
for my fly and unzipped it with surprising eagerness. In a
moment we were rolling on the cot, pulling at each other.
We kissed and my tongue went deep into her mouth. Her
hand moved up the inside of my thigh, passing lightly over
the groin. We were breathing hard. She sat up on my legs
and I entered her as she dug her fingers into my chest. Then
she rode up and down as I drove in, hungry as a starving
man at the proverbial banquet. It had been three months,
after all. I slid my finger along her clitoris from the front
and she began to shudder, biting hard on my neck. This
wasn't like the whore I'd been with on a summer vacation

in France who wouldn't let me kiss her and fucked with her blouse on. This was the real thing. Or seemed to be.

She came three times, then I did too, our fluids mingling on the sheets. After that we fell back and relaxed, closing our eyes for a few minutes. I felt like I was on a magic carpet. After a while, Cynthia got up and douched herself in a white enamel bowl.

"You really got into it," I said, watching her.

She smiled. "I like it. I get off on a lot of different men." She put down the bowl and walked over to me, touching my arm with the tips of her fingers. I grabbed her hand and held it.

"Why here?" I asked.

"Why not?" she answered, reaching under the end table, tossing me a baggie of a dark reddish grass, probably Panama, and some Marfil papers. I rolled a joint and passed it over. "In college I used to do it with guys just so they'd take me out to dinner. Now I do much better than that. Somebody's going to do it and it sure beats marriage."

I knew what she meant. She took a good hit on the grass and passed it back to me. I held it in as long as I could. On the wardrobe next to the incense, I could see a small photograph of a little girl. She might have been Cynthia's daughter.

"Where'd you go to school?" I asked.

"University of Denver. I was an art major. Mostly I posed."

"That's why you have the Lautrec."

"Yeah. You like Lautrec?"

I nodded.

"I used to think I was Jane Avril," she said, sitting next to me. "Jane Avril at the Moulin Rouge. Imagine that. But you can't be Jane Avril out here in the middle of the desert."

"Oh, I don't know."

We sat there a little longer, smoking the joint. Cynthia leaned over and looked at herself, primping in front of the mirror. *"Jane Avril avec ses hommes."*

I ran my hand down her back.

"Three atta time, Ralphie!" I heard the rancher shouting from the corridor. "You can do it." He crashed to the floor.

"Dumb bastard," said Cynthia, fingering the roach. "Drops $500 every time he comes here and then gets so drunk he can't even get it up. You should see him when he's angry." She laughed to herself, taking a final pull. A buzzer went off over the door jamb, flipping out a small paper flag. Cynthia turned to me and gave me a deep soul kiss. "Time's up, honey. Sorry." She reached down and tossed me my jeans, deftly stepping into her jumpsuit and zipping it up to the navel.

I stood and put on my clothes. She brushed the lint off my shirt. "Come again," she whispered in my ear. "I liked it. . . . Really." She opened the door and escorted me down the hall. I couldn't be sure whether she was telling the truth but it was more fun to accept it. Out in the waiting room, a drunken Naval officer was doing the hula in front of an Oriental girl. The mammy sat in the corner smoking a cigarette from a long red holder. Cynthia touched me on the cheek and returned to her room.

Inside the trailer, with the mood music and the colored lights, I had almost forgotten it was daytime; but walking out on the ranch grounds was like moving from a cattle car into a blast furnace. I wanted to take a running jump into the pond but held up under the watchful eye of the old cook. He was sitting under the tree with the swans at his feet.

"Want a room?" he asked.

"Room?"

"We've got rooms back there if you want to spend the night." He pointed over at the ranch house. "We've got rooms and we got a cafe, if you want bacon and eggs."

"I'm not hungry at the moment, thanks."

I slumped down opposite him in the shade of a desert ash. I still felt a buzz from the grass and wondered if it would help me solve the case, put the clues together as it sometimes could. I doubted it. Fifty yards away I could see an aluminum shed locked with a chain and combination. It had ventilation slats at the top and a pair of round portholes boarded over from the outside. Another fifty yards to the left a stone well stood in the shadow of an acacia.

I pushed myself up and walked in the direction of the shed. The cook got up and followed, lagging a few feet behind and studying me with his head at an odd tilt. He was a big man with the meaty hands of a field worker.

"Looking for something in particular?"

"No."

"Cause they don't like you walking around casual . . . that's not what it's for."

"It's a nice spread. Who owns it?"

He bent over and extracted an iron hoe from the bottom of a wheelbarrow. "I can't tell you that, mister, even if I wanted to."

"Alfred Craw?"

"Craw!" He spat on the ground in contempt.

"Sorry I asked."

I veered away from the shed in the direction of the acacia bush. A mangy dog ran across my path, disappearing behind the ranch house. I could hear a squawking from the chicken coop, the cry of the hens echoed by the hissing swans. At the other end of the oasis, some Mexicans were tending the date palms. They wore white handkerchiefs tied around their foreheads.

I approached the well. A circle of wooden planks surrounded its crumbling walls. A metal bucket hung from a rusty cable. I peered down into the water. It was limpid, pure spring water—clear at the top and descending into blackness. My reflection was sharp, the details of my face as precise as in a fine mirror. But the water was deep, endless. A stone dropped straight down would go forever, maybe emerge on the other side of the globe.

"You won't find nothin' in there." The reflection of the cook appeared next to mine. His expression was impassive. "Unless you're looking for fish."

I turned to him. "What fish?"

"Prehistoric fish. From when Death Valley was a lake."

"They're not alive?"

"Some of 'em. Up near the surface in underground tributaries where the water ain't too hot. The Navy sent down frogmen a few years back to catch the buggers . . . but they got trapped in a cave and ran out of air. Still floatin' around in there, I reckon." The cook rubbed his chin with his wrist.

"The fish or the frogmen?"

"Both."

Fish? It was hard to believe anything was alive under the desert. I squinted, staring hard into the depths, seeing visions in the murky water—dark prehistoric monsters with weird antennae protruding from their heads, human corpses bobbing in liquid like Halloween apples, the skin eroded, the fish nibbling at the dangling flesh. And then faces, gazing up at me, Lila Shea calling out and receding into the well, the brown arm of Luis Vazquez reaching upwards, a black box of bones inscribed PROPERTY OF THE CORONER'S OFFICE, the words fading away like the fortune at the bottom of a toy eight ball. The sound of an airplane interrupted my reverie, first a dull puttering sound, then something louder, more than a hobbyist out for a ride or a few friends in a Piper or a Mooney come to get laid. The shadow of the wings streaked over the desert. The reflection flashed across the surface of the well. I looked over at the landing strip to see a Lear jet bounce over the ground on its thick rubber wheels and taxi over toward the hangar. The big plane made three passes back and forth before it came to a halt. I stepped away from the well.

"Who's that?" I asked, but the cook didn't answer.

The pilot got out of the plane and opened the door for two men in business suits. The one in front carried a large grey attaché case. They walked together, eyes straight ahead, along the gravel path between the ranch and the airstrip. They didn't turn as they passed the silver Airstream trailer with its windows of gelatin and the pond with the weeping willow tree and the hissing swans. They continued along the path where it branched through the cottonwoods to the other side of the ranch house. I watched for a moment and then set out after them.

"You can't go there," said the cook, coming up behind me with the hoe swinging at his side.

"Why not?" I asked without looking back at him.

"It's off-limits to guests." He slid the hoe across the gravel in front of me, hooking it around my legs.

"How come?"

"Because that's the way it is."

"That's not a very good reason," I said, stepping sharply on the end of the hoe and making it fly into the air. As he watched, I slammed him hard in the gut. He buckled and clutched his stomach. I grabbed the hoe and held it over his head, threatening to come down on his skull. He looked up slowly.

"Turn around," I said. "Now march over behind the acacia there." I gave him a little kick in the pants for prodding. When we reached the other side of the bush, I raised the hoe higher over my head. "Sorry, old-timer," I said and brought it down on the back of his neck. He buckled at the knees and crashed into the dirt. A light trickle of blood flowed from the top of his cranium. I really was sorry. I bent down over him. He was out cold, but seemed all right. I untied his cook's apron and ripped it in pieces, using the parts to bind his legs and arms. Then I tied his whole body to the base of the bush and stuffed the bonnet of his chef's hat in his mouth.

I crawled out from behind the bush and followed the path leading around the ranch house. A manicured lawn had been planted in the front yard, necessitating an elaborate sprinkler system with rotating nozzles that gushed water like the Trevi Fountain. I kept out of the spray, close to the wall of the house. Inside, the traditional ranch style had been carefully preserved. Rough-hewn beams supported a stucco ceiling. An antique spinning wheel stood opposite a brick fireplace beneath a shelf lined with kachina dolls. A meeting was taking place in the next room. The door was ajar and I could see the back of one of the businessmen seated at an oak table, his attaché case leaning against his chair.

I continued along the wall to another angle. A series of frame windows opened out from the meeting room, but they were all shuttered. I peeked into the cracks but all I could see was a side view of the businessman with the attaché case. He was lifting it onto the table and opening the latch.

"Twelve to five," I heard a voice coming from the other side of the room. "Twelve to five. That's the Greek's morning line. It hasn't budged in a week."

"Fine. I just heard he has a habit of changing it at the last minute," said the man with the attaché case.

"So what?"

"So we lost out. That's all."

"Don't worry about it, Mat. Our bets go in this afternoon. After that he can switch the odds around to thirty to one Dillworthy, for all we care." Someone laughed. "Let's see the goods."

The man named Mat pushed his case across the table. It was lined with freshly minted bills, twenties and fifties.

"Don't forget the covering bet on Hawthorne," contin-

THE BIG FIX

ued the voice on the other side. "Forty-five thousand. Then we put the rest on Dillworthy without raising eyebrows."

The group fell silent.

I backed away from the wall. The front door was locked but I wondered if there were some way to get inside the house unnoticed. Ducking low, I circled around the side looking for a grate that might lead into the basement. There wasn't any. The windows were all sealed tightly. The kitchen door had been bolted shut. Behind a flower trellis, a drain-pipe led up to the roof. I grabbed hold of it and tugged. The pipe weakened at the joint, but I pulled myself up on it anyway, testing its give. A piece of siding slipped under my foot and slid to the ground. I froze against the building, feeling ridiculous and baking in the heat. Then I reached for the roof gutter and chinned myself, scrambling onto the roof and making an awful racket on the tile. Even up here the spray from the sprinkler still rose above me. It made a rainbow in the sun.

I looked around. The attic window I had planned on entering was nailed to the frame; there didn't seem to be other openings. I crawled across the roof to the air condi-tioner. A steady blast of hot air was coming out of the ex-haust. I lifted off the grid and placed it on the tile beside me. Then I spun on my haunches and pushed my feet through the duct. My skin burned from the exhaust. It felt like the heat would sear the soles off my shoes. But I pro-ceeded down anyway, pushing off at the top and wriggling along on my back like an upside-down snake.

In the dining room, the discussion had resumed. I could hear them talking, but against the whir of the air condi-tioner it was hard to make out the precise words. Something about cash flow. The odds were repeated in a boisterous voice I hadn't heard before. It was difficult to tell how many of them there were.

The duct widened and I was able to move more easily.

I turned myself over and inched forward. Eppis, Eppis, were you working with these people? After all those years of protest had it come to this? A cheap pay-off for a big fix. I drew near the vent over the meeting, but I didn't want to look.

And then the air conditioner stopped. Everything got very quiet except for a baseball game on a television set somewhere across the house. It was switched off.

"He's up there, all right!" came a voice.

"Who?"

"Check up on the roof. . . . Jonas, try that way."

I didn't move.

I heard feet racing across a hardwood floor.

"He's down here!"

"What the—?"

I saw fingers reaching through the grate. A .45 calibre revolver swung out from a shoulder holster.

Down below, Procari, Sr., stood there, holding his dark glasses in his hand and staring at me.

"Good to see you, Mr. Wine."

19

MEMORIES OF CHILDHOOD. Sonya and me, age six, walking along the boardwalk in Coney Island eating buttered corn and bialys.

A baseball game in Ebbets Field with Duke Snider in center and Erskine pitching.

The first day at school in Midwood High looking for the girl with long black hair from Grand Central Parkway. The ammonia smell in the cafeteria.

A quiet day in Berkeley playing chess with a guy named Al over on Northside.

Suzanne and me, making love for the first time on the beach in Carmel, the sand seeping into our sleeping bag from behind.

My head bashed by a cop at the LBJ riot in front of the Century Plaza Hotel.

Cynthia dancing the can-can with Alora at an old Parisian nightclub.

Then nothing.

I tried to move but I had no reflex, no will. A failure in the central nervous system. The synapses would not bridge.

I heard a noise. What was it? Humming. An airplane?

No. Shuffling. Scraping. I listened again. It became dimmer. But had the source receded or was it just me fading away again?

Then I awoke, the noise returning. Closer this time. More distinct. I felt a dull thud on my cheeks. A pressure on my jaw bone. Someone was slapping me.

"Wine! . . . Wine!"

I sat up, blinking, trying to focus. A face blurred in front of my eyes. I fell back against the wall, feeling burning metal with my hands. I was in the shed.

"Wine?"

It was Sebastian. His face was flushed, his forehead covered with red blotches. He was seated on the floor opposite me in his pajamas. They were torn across the sleeve.

"What'd they do to me?"

"Pentothal."

I shook my head. "What time is it?"

"Eight o'clock. Twilight." He pointed up at the vent over my head, where a slice of darkening sky was barely visible. Outside I could imagine a desert sunset, the ranch suffused with orange and red, the long shadows.

"So your father found you after all," I said.

"He always knew where I was."

"That figures. Like father, like son. Two rotten bastards. . . . What'd you do with Eppis?"

"Eppis?"

"Yeah, Eppis. Howard Eppis. Remember him?"

"Eppis is dead."

"You mean you murdered him, you dirty son of a bitch."

I stood, still groggy from the drug, pulling myself up.

"I didn't kill him. It was an accident."

"Accident, my ass." I lashed out at him, tripping over a saw horse and falling onto my side. My face brushed against the cement floor.

Sebastian bent over me. "Take it easy," he said. My

stomach began to hurt again and I grabbed at it, wrapping my arms around my rib cage. "That stuff's strong. It didn't wear off me for twenty-four hours."

"You?" I took a swing at him but I missed by a mile.

"They gave it to me yesterday when they brought me out here."

"Who brought you out here?"

"My father."

"Your father?" I looked at him again. He had been beaten badly. His lips were bruised and there was a long diagonal cut over his left eye. His nose had been pushed to the side. "Let's start over," I said. "Eppis is dead."

"Right."

"By an accident?"

"Yeah. . . . I think."

"You think? Was it an accident or wasn't it?"

"I'm not sure."

"You're not sure?"

"He knew too much. My father had to close the business."

"What business?"

"The Church. The Church. I was the Priest and my father ran the business end. I never wanted to do it in the first place."

I took a deep breath. Or tried to. Events were moving a little fast for me. Outside I could hear the sound of an airplane arriving. Some cars bounced down the dirt road, honking at each other. At sundown activity was picking up around the trailer.

"You're confusing me," I said. "You mean your father supported your Satanism."

"Yes."

"That's not what I heard."

"That was a cover. It was a racket and he set me up in it."

"What kind of a racket?"

"A cover for gambling clubs. Big-time. 23 Columbia Drive was going to be one of them. Everywhere there was a church there would be a club. Religions are always tied in with business. Like bingo. Why couldn't it be big-time gambling? That was his plan anyway, until Eppis found out."

"So your father had him killed."

"I don't know. He told me it was an accident. Drug overdose." Sebastian's voice cracked. He was trying to stop himself from crying. "My father was always doing things like that, telling me what to do. I suppose I wanted him to ... at least until Eppis died. I thought maybe he'd get off my back, that homicide was out of his league, but ..." Sebastian's voice cracked again. His eyes filled with tears.

"But what?" I asked.

"He used it against me, like he always did. When I started working for Hawthorne he set up this fix. Just to make himself another bundle gambling. At first I didn't even know where it was coming from, but then ..." He trailed off and looked away from me.

"How big is the bet?"

"Ten million. He asked me to help him. I told him I wouldn't until ..."

"Until what?" I tried to get up.

"Until he forced me. He made me make phone calls, like the one to you, pretending to be Eppis, telling them I supported Hawthorne just to prove he was alive. I could always mimic voices, ever since I was a boy." He sat on a box and put his head in his hand. "I wanted you to find out. Honest I did. I just didn't have the guts. . . . I wrote the letter myself so you would know about the explosion. . . . He's my father, after all."

A tear rolled down Sebastian's cheek.

"Why did he kill Lila Shea?"

"She suspected Eppis was dead. So did Luis Vazquez."

"Luis Vazquez? He knew Eppis was dead too?"

"He wasn't sure, but he thought so. He kept asking around for him."

"And you told your father about that?"

He nodded, looking away.

"What happened to Vazquez?"

"I don't know. . . . I don't know. I'm not sure."

"Not sure?! Like you weren't sure if Eppis' death was an accident?"

Sebastian sobbed. I couldn't figure whether he was lying or not. I leaned against the wall and slumped down opposite him.

"You know your father tells it differently," I said. "He says everything you did was to humiliate him. That every time he tried to help you, you turned him down, insulted him."

"I wish I had. He ruined my mother's life too, you know."

"Is your mother still alive?"

"It doesn't make any difference. She's a wreck of a woman and he did it."

"And you never wanted revenge on him, never wanted to get back or even kill him?"

"No. I was too weak."

"What about Skull and Bones. You came on pretty strong with the note and the dead rat on the pillow."

"Skull and Bones? Is he still talking about that? I could never have been in Skull and Bones. He took me out of Yale six months before Tap Night. It's in the records." Sebastian reached out and touched my sleeve.

"Wine, I swear to you. I didn't mean this. I wanted Hawthorne to win. I worked for him because it meant something to me."

"If what you're saying is true, how come your father left me here with you to hear the whole story?"

"Because it doesn't matter anymore. He can keep you locked in until it's all over and then get rid of you. Arrange another accident. There's no way out. As for me, he'll take me and give me a new identity someplace, just like he always does. Maybe South America. Maybe Europe. He trusts me."

"Should he?"

Sebastian didn't answer. He wouldn't look in my eyes.

I stood up and walked across the shed, pacing it off like a prisoner in a cell. His story confused me. It was a pathetic tale on the face of it, filled with self-pity, and Sebastian was playing it to the hilt. Maybe he had a right to, I wasn't sure, but relationships like this often had their own economy, a price exacted from each of the principals or a tension generated by a third party who had created the conflict. Whatever the case, I was in no mood to figure it out. I was locked in a shed in the middle of Death Valley with the success of the big fix assured and my head swimming with the prehistoric fishes. The more difficult it became, the more important Hawthorne's victory seemed to me. I was suckered. Already in my mind he had assumed the proportions of a Lao Tse, a great spiritual leader to lead our nation out of darkness.

"Do you know where the explosion will be?" I asked.

"The intersection of Hollywood and the Habor Freeways. Near the Music Center. At 3:00 A.M."

Only five hours.

"Who's going to do it? Jonas?"

"He and some others."

"How do they plan to tie in Eppis?"

"Letters have been sent to all major newspapers and television stations under Eppis' signature taking responsibility for the act and reaffirming his support for Senator

Hawthorne. They will arrive tomorrow morning, a few hours after the explosion."

"And what happens if people start investigating? If they discover Eppis is no longer alive?"

"By that time the election will be ancient history."

He had a point.

I shook my head, trying to clear the Pentothal. Ignoring the numbness, I piled two metal crates against the wall and climbed up to the vent. Peering out, I could see the old timer seated opposite the shed. He had a shotgun in his hand. To his right, the sun was slipping down behind the Panamints, bidding its last farewell to the desert and giving his face a somber ochre cast. I stood there watching for a few moments when I heard a cry from in front of the trailer.

"C'mon, girl, what kind of a diddly-shit desert fleabag you runnin' here?" It was the rancher. "All I'm asking is for you to stay in Barstow for a week. At the Arabian Nights Motel. They got color teevee in every room big as a cow's ass." He was reeling about in front of Cynthia who had changed into a suede skirt and tie-dye blouse. "Come on, honey," he said, stumbling toward her. "You look just like my own daughter run off to San Francisco five years ago. Pretty little thang wearing beads and all."

"Sorry, sweetie." She stepped away from him and ducked back into the trailer.

"Well, hot shit to you!" said the rancher.

The old-timer, sitting near him, started to laugh.

"What're you smilin' at?" The old man shook his head. "Better keep your smiles to yourself or I'll shove that shotgun up your nose."

The old-timer shrugged.

"Hey." I cupped my hands and shouted through the vent. "You should have heard what that bastard said about you." The rancher spun around looking for the source of the voice.

"Up here," I said.

He walked over to the shed. Only half my face was visible in the vent and it took him a moment to recognize me. "Hey, old buddy," he said. "What're you doin' up there?"

"Just messin' around."

He clapped his hands together. "Goddamn, they got you all locked up . . . What you been doin' to them who-ers?"

"Listen, did you hear what that bastard was saying about you?" I nodded in the direction of the old-timer who turned ominously in my direction, cocking his shotgun in warning.

"What'd he say?" said the rancher, putting his ear close to the shed.

I whispered to him: "He said the reason you come here is because your wife is always sleeping with the ranch hands."

"He said that?"

"Yup."

"He was kidding, of course."

"The hell he was." I paused meaningfully. The rancher turned away from me and stared at the old-timer. "You know what else he said?" I continued. "That your son isn't even yours. That your wife went to live with a man named Peterson in San Bernardino in 1948."

"That's a lie!" The rancher's skin blotched around his forehead.

"Well, you better tell him." I nodded again in the old man's direction. "He said it right in front of your boy."

"He did?" The rancher stormed over to where the old-timer was sitting. "What kind of bullshit were you handing out, fella?"

"Nothin', mister. I didn't say nothin'. You're not worth it anyway."

"What're you talkin' about, you old fart?" The rancher

wrenched the shotgun out of his hand and threw it across the ground.

"Your boy was sure upset," I added. "He was running all over looking for you."

"He was?" The rancher picked up the old-timer by the collar. "You rotten bastard!" he said and hit him in the chin with a solid right. The old-timer shot straight up into the air, then fell over on his side. His eyes had the glazed look of a boxer's after the third knockdown. I was beginning to worry about him.

"Son of a beehiver," said the rancher, marching away from him toward the trailer. "Ralph . . . Ralph Murchison, come on out here, boy! I've got something to tell ya." He stepped up to the door.

"Hey, uh, Mr. Murchison. . . . Mr. Murchison."

"Yah?"

"Before you go in there, could you do me a small favor . . ."

"What's that?"

"Get me out of here."

"Can't. It's a combination lock."

"Well, shoot it off." I pushed my hand through the vent and pointed toward the shotgun.

He looked at me for a moment. "Okay, buddy," he said with a grin. "But don't you be givin' any of them who-ers a bad time, now. They're nice girls." He picked up the gun and aimed it at the door.

"Wait a minute!" I shouted, motioning to Sebastian to hug the wall. "All right."

The rancher fired, blowing the door open on its hinges. The shed filled with dust. I walked outside.

"Thanks, Mr. Murchison."

"Anytime, old buddy." He headed toward the trailer. "Ralph . . . Ralph Murchison, come out here this minute!"

"So long, Sebastian," I said. The gambler's son was slumped in a corner of the shed. I was nervous about what could happen to him but I had no time for that now.

I crossed the gravel path around the pond. I guessed it was just past 10:00 and with some luck I might be back in Los Angeles to stop the bombing if they waited until 3:00 like they were supposed to. I sat down in the Buick and found my spare keys in the magnetic box under the radio. I turned the ignition. Nothing. Again: No contact. No spark, no brake light, no radio, nothing. I got out of the car and opened the hood. Someone had taken a hammer to the engine. The block was smashed, the generator broken in two. Procari planned ahead.

I backed away from the car, feeling the Pentothal. Maybe I could telephone Los Angeles, but the lines in the ranch house were probably guarded. Then there were planes. Two men were seated in the cockpit of a Piper Cub, preparing to take off. "Hold it!" I shouted, running toward them. "Hold it!" But they couldn't hear me over the roar of the propeller. The Piper took off into the night, its red signal lights blinking against a black sky. The airstrip was empty.

I walked out further. If I kept going along the dirt road, I might be in Death Valley Junction by morning. Just in time to watch the news on the *Today* show at a rural cafe. Barbara Walters looking quite grave reciting the up-to-date totals of death and injury on the Harbor Freeway; an interview with someone important in the Hawthorne campaign.

"Does this damage the candidate's effort to woo the mainstream of American public opinion?" Perhaps even a statement from the boy wonder Nate Sugars: "Can your computer account for variables as extreme as this?" "The computer is not infallible, Mr. Newman. But whatever harm has been done, it will be counteracted at the polls on Tuesday. Senator Hawthorne will win. The voters know he is not capable of an act like this, even . . ."

"Even what? . . . Even if his supporters are?"

"I, uh, didn't say that, Mr. Newman. I doubt that this was the work of Hawthorne supporters. In fact, information we have leads us to believe . . ."

"Is that information verifiable, Mr. Sugars?"

"We're in the process of . . ."

"I see."

A commercial break to repair the normal traffic flow around the Los Angeles freeways. Cars are reported to be backed up as far as the La Tijera off-ramp and beyond.

I turned and headed back toward the trailer. Some of the farmworkers had returned from the date groves, creating a strange ecumenical atmosphere, a piquant mixing of the classes conducive to sex. I touched the seat of Murchison's Harley and continued past them to the side of the building. A yellow light was on in Cynthia's cubicle and the shade was drawn. I rapped on the glass. No response. I rapped again.

"Cynthia!"

She came to the window, pulling back the shade with a look of annoyance. Behind her, I could see the perplexed figure of a man holding his undershorts.

"Oh, it's you," she said.

"*Aristide Bruant dans son cabaret* at your service." I pretended to tip my hat like Maurice Chevalier in the old Lubitsch movie.

"If you come back later. . . ." she smiled.

"Can't. I'm in trouble."

"What?"

I stepped closer to the window. "I've got to get out of here."

"Hey! What's going on!" The man with the undershorts moved in toward the glass. He was young with short-cropped hair like fraternity boys used to have. "You got a boy friend or something?"

"What is it?" she asked.

"I'm up against it. That motherfucker of a rancher is threatening to kill me."

"He is?"

"Yeah. He's been storming around the ranch saying I told a lie about his son."

"You're the one?" she asked. Her naked breasts were pressed against the glass, flattening the nipples. "I thought he was after the cook."

"He wants me too. What do you think I should do?"

"Get the hell out of here before he shoots you."

"I can't. The bastard smashed my car."

She paused for a moment to think it over. "Sounds like you are in trouble."

"Damn right. Unless. . . ."

"Unless what?"

"Unless you get me the keys to his bike."

"Are you crazy?"

"No. Just slide your hand into his pocket and see if he stops you."

"Two weeks ago that bastard broke a girl's arm just because she laughed when he lost his hard-on."

"Cynthia, do you want my blood on your hands?"

"Look, Moses, you're a nice guy and all, but . . ."

The fraternity boy came up behind her, putting his arm around her neck and kissing her back. She made a resigned face at me. "Sorry," she said.

"Please, Cynthia. . . ."

The fraternity boy pulled the shade.

I walked to the other side of the pond, sitting down on the root of an ash which trailed off into the water. Across from me, the swans were asleep, their long necks bent with their beaks tucked under their wings. Time had run out. I listened to the sounds of the desert, the mocking cry of a thousand insects, and thought of Lila Shea. If she had only stayed away from Eppis. But that was always Lila's way, tripping around every little trend like it was the last flash of the century. And maybe Eppis wasn't so bad after all. He might have fallen for some dumb religion, but at least he had the brains to sense something rotten under the surface. That appeared to have cost him his life.

I gave up, slumping down and letting the reeds of the pond play in front of my eyes. A good breeze had come up and the temperature had cooled considerably.

Then I heard a rustling among the reeds. A rattling noise had awakened the swans. I leaned to my side. A set of keys was lying in the wet grass. The chain was attached to a gold medallion with the crest of the Barstow Grange. It was inscribed to Arthur P. Murchison for twenty years of service to the community.

"Have a nice ride," said Cynthia, standing at the edge of the pond.

20

F LAT OUT: LATHROP Wells, Johnnie, Pahrump and So-
shone. Tecopa Hot Springs, Ibex Pass and the Amar-
gosa River. Harley riding like a runaway horse.
Four-stroke vertical twin engine. 470 pounds dry weight.
My shirt pressed back hard against my chest. The wind beating down my throat. I hadn't been on a bike like this in
seven years.

Silurian Lake, Silver Lake, Baker. Joshua trees dancing
in the night, the road flapping like a flag, wheels bouncing
on the lane markers. Gas stations and cafes. Signs: JOHNNY
HORIZON SAYS: "THIS LAND IS YOUR LAND. KEEP IT CLEAN." I
stopped at a Holiday House outside of Barstow, wiring writing up on coffee and a half box of No-Doz. A headline on
the *Tri-City Express:* "Record Turn-out Predicted in Demo
Primary."

Back on the road, the Arabian Nights Motel blinking its
neon camel: NO VACANCY. And on to Victorville, Cajon Pass
and San Bernardino, not stopping to think, not watching for
the Highway Patrol, not worrying about crashing head over
heels, slamming splat like a child's mud pie into the center
divider. If Hawthorne won this election, I would exact my

price. The Oval Room would be changed to the Lila Shea Memorial Salon. One Jewish dick would have a pipeline to the White House.

Etiwanda, Cucamonga, Upland, the Los Angeles County Line and Claremont. Traffic was picking up, building to a climax, a crescendo of freeways. Santa Ana, Harbor, San Bernardino, 605, Long Beach, Garden Grove, Golden State coming together in off-ramps, underpasses, loops. The Water and Power Building looming in the distance like an electric waffle, fountains of pink and green like Versailles trivialized beyond description. The City of Angels, the basin the Indians called the Land of the Many Smokes.

I slowed in the right lane and turned off on Broadway into Chinatown. The streets were empty except for a small crowd in front of the Canton Bar spilling out into the courtyard of the Bank of Hong Kong. An electric clock was illuminated in the lobby of the bank. 2:30. The Harley purred softly beneath me, proud of its performance. I puttered around the block past a butcher shop and a large Chinese supermarket to an Oriental-style Shell Station with lion statues by the pumps and a Pagoda roof. I pulled into the station and made a phone call. Then I went on, driving up the hill on Yale Street and parking by the side of the freeway, fifty yards from the top. I got off the bike and walked the rest of the way, moving what I hoped was inconspicuously among the columns. The abutments of the Music Center were visible over the rise. I could see the reflecting pool and the relief on the Forum Theatre. Down below was the facade of a restaurant called The Little Executive, a lumberyard and a fire-station.

I leaned against a cement block. The area beneath the freeway was deserted and smelled of mulching grass. The cars roared over my head at a frequency of about one every half minute. At a location like this there was no ceasing, even in the small hours of the morning. I watched the access roads—the wide avenues coming from downtown and the side streets winding up from Chinatown. Temple Street ran off to my left, debouching at the far end of Union Station. Beside it, Sunset went as far as Olvera Street and the Pico Restorations, a dime-store version of Old Mexico reeking of moldy sugar cookies and stale guacamole. A bandstand occupied the center of the piazza where, four years ago, Bobby Kennedy had stood and received the accolades of a Latin American dictator. *Viva Bobby! Viva Bobby!*

My hands were clammy, sticking to the inside of my pockets like a used gum wrapper. A moving van rushed through the underpass and rattled the columns. I waited, wishing I had a weapon but knowing I wouldn't use it. The minutes inched forward, time fractured like a cannabis dream. Off in the distance a Volkswagen van pulled up and parked in front of the lumberyard. From the other direction, a solitary figure moved through the underpass on foot. I ducked back behind a column. He wore a dark suit and a handkerchief over his face. In his right hand he carried a black box. I watched as he walked to the end of the underpass and then turned, heading back again toward Temple Street.

Moments later two more men in handkerchiefs joined him, one of them carrying a second black box and the other a coil hooked over his shoulder. Together, the three men crouched down, heading beneath the low ceiling toward where the freeways intersected. The man with the coil let the end trail out behind, unfurling it as he went. When they reached the far wall, the men with the boxes placed them about fifty feet apart and began to attach the detonators.

I slid along the opposite wall to Temple Street. Looking down, I took off my jacket and signalled to the Volkswagen below. Six people climbed out of the van and started winding their way up the hill. They wore black robes and carried masks. I waved them on faster. Soon they were running.

The men looked up from their detonators. The one with the coil dropped his end and ran out into the street. He saw six figures wearing Aztec masks. They were moving swiftly toward him, chanting. Several of them held knives high over their heads. Alora was in front, her lovely body draped in an elaborate priestess robe, an Amazon on the attack.

"Watch it!" shouted the man with the coil.

His two buddies ran out on the street with him. One of them pulled a thirty-eight from inside his jacket, firing it down at the advancing Chicanos. They scattered into the neighboring buildings, one of them clutching his arm, the blood soaking through the black robe.

Then the three men turned, running off in the opposite direction, heading down the hill with two of the actors still pursuing them. At the next curb, the man with the gun tripped, flying into the pavement. Alora shouted. Her brother jumped on top of him, his knife held high over his head. In a flash, he plunged it into the man's rib, rolling him over and pulling him up by the collar. A stream of red liquid flowed into the sewer grate.

Later, we drove the van along a winding street in Elysian Park. I sat in the front clutching the black box while Jorge drove. His sister was directly beside me. I could feel her thigh against mine. In the back, one of their friends lay groaning on the floor, a tourniquet around his arm. At the stop sign we turned on Stadium Way toward Chavez Ravine.

"You are a very clever man," said Jorge. "Stopping this was very clever."

"Yeah, I know," I said, unable to generate much enthusiasm. "Real clever. You wouldn't believe how clever I am."

"What do you mean?" said Alora.

"I mean this," I said, opening the black box and removing a stick of dynamite. I held it up over her head and broke it open, snapping it at both ends. A clump of brown powder poured out onto the floor.

"Sand?" she said.

"Sand," I confirmed.

"Stupid bastard," said Jorge, pulling up at the gate of Dodger Stadium. The words GIANTS NEXT! were registered on the computerized sign across the parking lot.

"I came all the way back from Nevada for a dumb show ... what time is it?"

"3:35," said someone in the back.

"Somewhere in this city an explosion is taking place just about now," I said, but I wasn't thinking about it. I was thinking about Sebastian, about why he had lied about the location of the bombing. Had it been deliberate or had his father kept him confused as well? I couldn't figure it. By now it was probably academic anyway.

"Well, Mr. Detective," said Jorge. "Where do we go from here?"

"I don't know."

"You don't know?! You bring us out here in the middle of the night, get Esteban a thirty-eight shell in his right arm for a bunch of sand, and you don't know? You got a lot to answer for, *gabacho*."

I didn't try.

I leaned against the window and stared out across the city. From this angle you could see the City Hall and the Municipal Court House, the Hollywood Freeway linking up with the San Bernardino. Any second I expected to see a flare. I didn't want to look. I slumped down in the seat of the van and closed my eyes, but the image of the city remained. I could trace the skyline with my fingers, the possible points of detonation. It would be impossible to cover them all in a month.

"Maybe they're bombing the Times building," I said. "That one cost Los Angeles a socialist mayor in 1911."

"Big fucking deal," said Jorge. "Let's go home and get Esteban to a doctor."

He backed around the gate and headed out of the park in the direction of Riverside. I opened the window and took a deep breath of damp night air. A cloud cover had swept in from the ocean, totally obscuring the gibbous moon.

"No," I said. "Let's go back to the same place."

"Let's what?" said Jorge, staring hostilely at me. "Forget it. We've had enough for tonight." He turned and looked at his sister. "If there's one thing I can't stand, it's a *gabacho* who always thinks he's doing you a favor."

"Look," I said. "I'm not sure about this, but I think they were setting us up. They had reason to believe we might be on to them and they wanted to clear us out."

"What reason?" said Alora.

"I was in Nevada looking for this guy named Alfred Craw at the Palm Casino in Tonopah and ended up at some godforsaken place called Cottonwood Meadows. . . . It's too complicated. Do what you want." I sank down in the seat again and gazed at my knuckles. It would have been a last resort anyway.

"Good," said Jorge. "Why don't you get out here." He stopped the car and opened the door for me.

Before I could move Alora leaned forward and took her brother by the arm. "Esteban's all right," she said.

"So what?"

"So what?" she repeated, shaking her head at him. "So *no hay tiempo para hablar. Ve al centro como dice.*" She spoke with the authority of a stage director.

"It's stupid," said her brother, but he circled around again and turned onto the Golden State going downtown. Traffic was light. In less than a minute the Music Center appeared ahead of us again. Slowing down, we veered off through Chinatown and came up the same way behind the Shell station and the supermarket. Jorge parked in front of an insurance office near where the man had been knifed.

His body had been removed from the sewer grate. The area beneath the underpass was empty. They had left.

"See," he said. "Gone. That's it."

"I don't think so," I said, opening the door and dismounting from the van. The others watched me as I pointed over the freeway bridge to the Forum Theatre. A wide banner had been strung along the facade—

HOWARD EPPIS AND THE FREE AMERIKA PARTY
BACK
HAWTHORNE IN '72

The message was printed in bold red letters, visible for half a mile. Howard holding a rifle and brandishing a fist appeared at the bottom, a public nightmare of the 1960's brought to life at the intersection of the Hollywood and the Santa Ana Freeways, the dreams of one decade degraded by the next.

I took a few steps forward and drew an imaginary line from the banner to the bridge. Then I motioned for them to follow me. Leaving one man with Esteban, the five of us proceeded up the hill at the base of the underpass by a row of newly-planted succulents. Peering down Temple Street, the sidewalks were bare. A woman walked her dog on the plaza of the Music Center. No one talked. We continued, single file, along the freeway abutment, listening for voices, listening for the burning sizzle of a fuse. At the corner of Temple and Grand, we turned up the off-ramp, but froze at the entrance. Something about stepping on the surface of the freeway, a taboo of sorts, held us back.

Then we all saw it together, a keg of dynamite standing in the middle of the freeway like some graven icon implanted by a willful god. A detonation wire ran off in the opposite direction. The cars dodged around it, seemingly unaware of its content, mistaking it perhaps for a barrel of cement mix left over by a crew of careless road workers.

We waited for a lull in the traffic, wandering about the detonation wire, and the source of its connection on the other side of the abutment. A flatbed truck sped by, stacked with Pontiac sedans followed by a trio of milk trucks from a dairy in Orange County. After they were gone, the five of us crouched low and dashed across the freeway, clutching eagerly for the center divider. We heard a hissing sound from over the abutment.

"Corta-lo hombre," said Alora to her brother, who held his knife at shoulder height.

Jorge reached down and sliced the wire from the keg. *"Suerte!"*

Down below, a Ford pickup backed up with a screech and roared up Temple Street toward Figueroa. It was the same car I had seen tearing out of Hawthorne headquarters when I had first visited there with Lila Shea.

21

YOU SAID HE was still alive!" Jorge insisted angrily.
"Well, I, uh..." We carried the dynamite keg around the running track circling Echo Park Lake. A grove of palm trees filled a tiny island in front of us like a miniature Banana Republic. "I, uh, can't be sure."

"Then why'd you tell me that on the phone?"

"I needed help. There wasn't time."

"So he's dead."

"I didn't say that either."

"Make up your mind, *gabacho*." This time it was Alora. Her eyes were dark and accusative. It made me nervous. "Is Luis Vazquez alive or is he dead?"

"I don't know."

She shook her head in disgust.

"*Ay, pindejo!*" said Jorge, dropping the dynamite on the track. We all jumped backwards. "I don't want to carry this stuff anymore." He pushed with his foot and rolled the keg into the water. It made a large splash and floated on the surface.

"You should have cut a hole in it first," said Alora.

"Shut up."

We stood there for a moment watching the dynamite float off into the middle of the lake. Soon it began to sink.

"See what I mean," said Jorge.

Alora folded the Hawthorne banner around some rocks and dropped it after the dynamite keg. It sank quickly to the bottom. Some kid would probably bring up a piece of it catfishing over the summer.

"What about this man Procari?" she said. "Does he know where my father is?"

"If anybody does."

"Where does he live?"

"In Rolling Hills."

"Where?"

"A rich neighborhood out by the ocean."

"And you think he's keeping my father there?"

"I doubt it. He wouldn't hide anyone in his own house."

"Then where?"

"Who knows. Maybe in a castle."

"A castle?"

I nodded. "That's a good place to hide people . . . a castle. Good facilities."

"And where's this castle?" she asked. "England or France?" She had a bemused, skeptical expression that made me want to grab her and forget the castle and Procari and her father and anybody else for that matter.

"Somewhere north of Sunset and west of La Cienega. It belongs to Isabel La Fontana."

"Who's she?"

"I think she was Procari's wife."

22

THE LIGHTS WERE off in most of the houses as we drove up Queen's Way to Isabel La Fontana's. Only the upstairs of an A-frame was illuminated with a man pacing about his bedroom in a terry-cloth robe. At La Fontana's a thick privet hedge obscured the Norman facade. In passing it was difficult to see if anyone was awake. We continued on, parking near the corner of Mulholland fifty yards beyond, and returned on foot, four of us—Jorge, Manuel, Alora and me. When we reached her house, the entry light was out and the gate in front of the moat was padlocked. On the other side, we could see the German shepherds asleep, snoring quietly.

We circled around to the side, across the lawn of a Tudor mansion, staring up at the parapets. The upper windows were shuttered. No light was visible through the cracks. We walked around to the back of the castle. The moat ended abruptly and the manner of construction changed to simple stucco as if the builders gave up their medieval pretext *in medias res*, deciding it was too pretentious even for the Sunset Hills. Or too expensive. The rear of the house was flimsy and motel-like, slatted with louvred windows like a middle class tract. The Ford pickup was parked under the acrylic carport.

We heard a woman crying. Her sobs came through the louvres.

"Don't do it," she said. "Don't do it, Oscar. . . . Please."

La Fontana.

I crept up to the window. The woman was half-sitting, half-lying on the floor with her face in her hands and her forehead almost touching the hardwood. Her hair was bedraggled, her skin flaked and wrinkled. She looked seventy years old.

Procari stood opposite, flanked by Jonas and the other heavy. Jonas had his gun in his hand, but he wasn't pointing it at her. In the far corner, Sebastian sat slumped on a sofa, his face ashen.

"What do you want, Isabel?" said Procari. "A ten million dollar loss?"

"Ten million dollars to you."

"You lost too, Isabel!"

"I don't care."

"You don't care? I let you in on this as a favor. Ever since I closed the Church you've been whining about how poor you are. You'd think you were on food stamps."

"You can't make the boy do something like that."

"Boy? He's thirty-three years old." Procari lifted a telephone from the end table and carried it over to the sofa, handing the speaker to his son. "743-4000. Ask for the night editor."

"What do I say?" asked Sebastian.

"What I told you. Tell him you're Eppis and the letter you sent to the *Times* was incorrect. An oversight. You meant the morning of June 1, not May 31."

"I don't know if I can do it, dad," said Sebastian. His face was going through a peculiar twitching motion that was difficult to watch.

Procari turned to Jonas. "You dial it."

Jonas leaned down and began to dial the number, but midway through he was interrupted by a loud yelp. The German shepherds were tearing around the house straight at us. The first one jumped high in the air, landing on Manuel. The other lunged at Alora's leg. Before I could make a move, her brother pulled his knife and slashed at the dog's neck. On the second thrust, the blood spurted out like a fountain in front of the rear window. The other dog retreated in terror, barking hysterically.

"Once again, Mr. Wine." Procari nodded to me from the back door. He was standing with Jonas and his buddy, both of whom now held guns on us, chest high. They signalled for us to raise our hands.

"Mr. Wine," Procari continued, "gentlemen and lady, will you step back a few feet." We stepped backwards as the three men followed us into the yard. Procari bent over to look at the slain shepherd. His mate whimpered in the background. "Miss La Fontana will be most distressed at the condition of her dog. He was a champion, you know. He won the blue ribbon at the Western States Kennel Show in San Diego. Champion Hermes Trismegistus. A rather pathetic name, don't you think, Mr. Wine?"

"Tacky."

Jonas jabbed his gun deep in my ribs. "Just like Oscarino and his absurd identification with King Nestor," Procari went on. "The powerless always have a strong attraction for the occult, but I suppose you know that, Moses."

"Your son didn't want to be King Nestor, Procari... anymore than Howard Eppis wanted his bones ending up in a little black box in the Coroner's office."

"Good guess, Mr. Wine. Excellent. I compliment you." La Fontana emerged from the back door making a valiant effort to hold herself erect, but she had the frail, wavering stance of a morphine addict. Procari turned and smiled at her. "Oscarino always was more Isabel's son, sickly and weak. He suffered from terrible asthma attacks when he was a child. Maybe if he hadn't always run to his mother, he would have grown into a real man."

"Tell me, Procari, did your son set me up for that fake at the freeway—or was it your own diabolical device?" It didn't matter. But I had to exercise restraint if we were getting out of this.

"My son is incapable of original action." La Fontana knelt down beside her dog and began to weep. I looked to my side.

"Keep still!" said Jonas.

I lunged at him, but he slammed me in the shoulder with his gun butt. I thought I heard a bone crack.

"You know, Mr. Wine," said Procari, "if you had had the good sense to remain at the Meadows, you wouldn't have forced me into sacrificing this new vehicle. I might have found a solution for you that was easier on both of us."

"Yeah, something outrageous like shooting me up with psilocybin and dropping me down that well."

"Get in there!" The two gunmen prodded us into the rear of the pickup. We didn't seem to have a choice.

Jonas closed the gate and locked it. I could feel Alora shivering next to me.

"Take them to Tujunga Canyon. . . . I'm sorry, Mr. Wine. But it's not only my money involved. I'm responsible to a lot of people, a cartel of sorts. We can't take risks."

"All my sympathy, Procari. I know you've always wanted to take care of those close to you."

Procari nodded and Jonas started around for the cab of the truck. This was it. I was trying to remember the words to the mourner's Kaddish.

Then I saw a dark figure looming up on the parapet. Like the ghost in Olivier's *Hamlet*, he raised his ancient weapon. For a split second I thought it was an illusion, the dazed outgrowth of twenty-four sleepless drug-crazed hours, but the weapon fired.

Procari fell to the ground, his cranium split, brains and blood mingling on the lawn as gory as a placenta.

Another shot.

This time the blast rammed Jonas into the rear of the truck.

The other thug dropped his gun and threw himself on the ground, screaming for mercy.

I climbed out of the truck and looked around.

Sebastian was standing at the back door, sobbing. "I had to let him out. I had to let him out," he said. "I couldn't do it myself."

Turning upwards, I saw the dark figure on the parapet more clearly. His face was creased and sallow as if he had spent a lot of time indoors.

Luis Vazquez threw his rifle to the ground.

23

I STARED THROUGH the window of the Rampart Division at the El Batey Market and the Cuban record store. The morning seemed to have been going on for hours. Forms, questions, explanations, interviews, autopsies—it was endless. My shoulder throbbed. My head was beginning to feel like the inside of a steam press. Evidently Craw and some Vegas cronies had placed a large bet on Dillworthy in the name of Monarco Enterprises. Monarco Enterprises was owned by Caracoa Industries, a subsidiary of Golfo Imperial Limited, which was in turn controlled by Apellido Feo, S.A., a holding company Procari had set up in Venezuela. To come full circle, there was no Alfred Craw. That was a pseudonym Procari used for the Board of Directors of Monarco Enterprises. It was all very boring. When Koontz indicated he was about to wrap it up, I broke into a broad grin. At that point I would have done anything to get out of there.

"As I see it, there's no point in the newspapers hearing about this case," said Koontz, leaning across his desk and fingering his umpteenth cigar.

"Suit yourself," I said. A warrant for my arrest had been crumpled into a ball and thrown into the wastebasket.

"Now, just a minute," said Sugars, who was sitting next to me. "The way I see it, the public has a right to know. Certain parties, possibly allied to Governor Dillworthy, possibly not, but in any case working in his behalf, were attempting to smear Senator Hawthorne for their own financial gain, defrauding the voters and causing the deaths of several persons."

"Uhuh," said Koontz. "That's the way you see it, is it?"

"Right."

"Well, that's what I always thought about you pseudo-liberals. Opportunists. Every time a cop shoots a Mexican, it's manslaughter; every time a Mexican shoots a cop, it's social justice."

"Not social justice, Koontz," I said. "Good marksmanship."

"So you condone the wanton murder of police officers, is that it?"

"Oscar Procari wasn't a cop, Koontz." Sugars was mad. I was restless.

Koontz snorted and doused his rum crook in the ashtray. "Look, I don't want to bullshit with you. I heard enough about your kind in my propaganda course at USC. As far as I'm concerned, this case is closed. If you want to reopen it, that's your affair. But I promise you when those press boys come snooping around here, I'm gonna deny the whole thing and create enough confusion to make it look bad until the election."

Sugars shrugged in resignation.

"If this interview is over," I said, "I think I'd like to catch up on my sleep." I started for the door.

"Not so fast, Wine," said Koontz, reaching in his drawer for a slip of paper. "There's a little matter of a defective tail light which, according to our records, has not been repaired. This is an impound order on your car, Buick, license number RLT786."

"I don't want to obstruct justice. You can find it off a dirt road 23 miles out of Death Valley. Just bring a tow truck. The engine's wrecked and the back wheels are gone."

I dropped the keys on the desk in front of him.

"Nobody likes a smart ass, Weinberg, but you know what?"

"What?"

"I feel sorry for you."

Sugars and I left the police station together. It was hot outside. The smog was heavy for the last day in May and I shielded my eyes from the sun as we walked down the steps. At the bottom, Sugars turned toward the station parking lot.

"I never would have guessed Eppis was dead." He stopped and looked up at the sky. "Oh, I almost forgot," he said, reaching into his pocket for an envelope. "Here's your money and a ticket to the Hawthorne victory party at the Beverly Hills Hotel."

"You can keep the ticket," I said, returning it to him. "I like to endure the elections in private. It's a tradition with me. Besides, I'm not very good at celebrating. . . . Give it to Sebastian. He'd like it."

"Sebastian?"

"Yeah, the poor demented bastard's been feeling low since he was three years old. I think it would cheer him to feel wanted at the victory party. He really supported Hawthorne, you know."

"That's what you said. . . . Say, I've been wondering— how did you know Isabel La Fontana was Sebastian's mother?"

"It was a hunch. Isabel La Fontana was the stage name of an actress who used to do impressions at night clubs on the Strip during the fifties. She went on with her teen-age son who could also mimic—Jimmy Cagney, Jerry Lewis, that kind of thing. Sebastian was good. He had Eppis' voice down to a tee—or almost. So when he started to whine about what had happened to his mother. . . ."

"You guessed she was the one."

I nodded.

He reached for the handle of a rented Oldsmobile loaded with Hawthorne posters. "Can I give you a lift someplace? Sure must be a bitch to be without wheels in this town." The last sentence was a little colloquial for him, but he managed it okay.

"No thanks. I've got a ride," I said, pointing to Alora waiting across the street in the front of her Studebaker. She looked great against the flaking blue paint. I waved and started across without looking back at Sugars. There was something about the whiz kid that still turned my stomach.

"How's your father?" I asked, slipping in beside her.

"Fine. He's sleeping."

She smiled and kissed me lightly om the lips.

"That's good," I said.

Alora started the car and we drove over to Barragan's for huevos rancheros, sitting there for a while, talking and drinking Dos X's. After that we went over to my place and stretched out on the couch to listen to some Valerie Simpson. Then Scott Joplin. It was a nice afternoon. In a few hours I even forgot about being tired.

24

A S PROMISED, I spent Election Night home with the kids. The three of us sat cross-legged on the floor with a bowl of popcorn before us, our eyes glued to CBS. For a while, anyway. Throughout the evening Simon had remained transfixed by Walter Cronkite's jowly contortions, but Jacob hated them all. He stood up and walked in front of the set, blocking the screen.

"News," he said. "All grown-ups like is news."

"What's wrong with that?"

"News is yucky. I wanna watch cartoons."

"There aren't any cartoons on," I said, but he didn't move from the set, watching me distrustfully. "Look, Jacob," I tried to reason with him. "This isn't just the news. Tonight is an important night. Tonight they are trying to decide who's running for President."

"Aunt Sonya says elections are the opium of decadent democracy."

"Move away from the screen."

"No," he said, holding tight to the chassis.

"You're gonna get it."

"Madas says people who watch the news have bad karma."

"Madas can fuck himself!" He probably could, too.

I grabbed Jacob around the waist and pulled him down on the floor. "Now listen, punk. You're staying right here until the last precinct in the last district has reported all its votes. Or else . . . or else . . . I'll shove your little head in the popcorn."

Jacob looked at me and started to cry. Five minutes later he had fallen asleep in my lap.

I sat through the night watching the votes come in. There weren't any surprises. Hawthorne won comfortably, if not extravagantly. At about 1:00 A.M. the victory party began. Balloons floated up to the ceiling of the Beverly Hills Hotel Ballroom as a bunch of dignitaries paraded in front of the cameras making dull pronouncements. After a sufficient period of suspense, the candidate appeared with his wife. Pandemonium reigned as a seven-piece combo played a forgettable campaign song composed especially for the occasion.

Hawthorne put up his hands for silence and began to speak. I didn't pay attention. My eyes were riveted on the audience, studying those wide camera angles of the ballroom, looking for Sebastian. Over on the dance floor, along the refreshment tables, under the colonnade—I couldn't find him. I saw Sugars, standing near the podium, waving a clipboard and yelling at a technician, but I never saw the county coordinator. Somehow I had wanted him to be there. But at least he was free of his old man after all these years. That was better.

I looked at Jacob asleep on my lap. And Simon curled up at the end of the sofa sucking his thumb. Being a father was a tough gig. I wondered if in some unconscious way I was warping my sons as surely as Procari had. I hoped not.

AFTERWORD

by

ROGER L. SIMON

The Big Fix was an accident.

The year was 1972. I was nearly broke, living in a rickety house in LA's Echo Park District with my then-wife and two baby boys, and I had just written a "serious" novel. Called *The Return*, it was a grim affair about a Cuban veteran of the Bay of Pigs who, on the tenth anniversary of that failed invasion, kidnapped the son of the radical lawyer who lived across the street and then proceeded to have a nervous breakdown for the next one hundred and fifty pages.

Not surprisingly, no one wanted to publish it—or at least no one my agent could locate on the planet Manhattan—and as a last act of desperation I gave it personally to my old editor, Alan Rinzler. He had just come West to start Straight Arrow Books, *Rolling Stone* magazine's new book publishing wing. Alan liked the novel, or claimed he did, but said he had to ask his financial guy to run his eyes over it, "just to be sure."

A few years later in Hollywood I would have known instantly what *that* meant, but I was gullible enough then to live with hope for a few days. The following week, Alan dashed it. We were sitting in my back yard, sharing the obligatory early-Seventies bomber, and he allowed as how things weren't going to work out for *The Return*. But he really wanted me to do something for his new company. Didn't I have any ideas that were "more *Rolling Stone*"?

Given my financial status, I knew I had to come up with something fast or my brilliant literary career was going to have a quick ending. So I started to improvise. I'd recently been reading a number of Raymond Chandler and Ross MacDonald detective thrillers, half for escapism and half because I thought they were the purest aesthetic expression of California life. Maybe I should do one of those but with a new twist, a hero who was more like Alan and me, a longhaired, draft-dodging, pot-smoking man of our crazy times. No one had done that before and it was definitely "Rolling Stone."

Perhaps it was the flattery—Who wouldn't want to see himself as a shamus? Will Bogart be playing me?—but Alan went for it. He asked me what I wanted to call my Philip Marlowe. "Moses Wine," I shot back without thinking because that was the hero of an autobiographical novel I had recently abandoned on page forty, liking nothing other than the name of the protagonist. He liked it, too.

And that was that. We made a contract and I just sat down and wrote. I had no idea what I was doing. I had never plotted a mystery before and hated doing detailed outlines. So I picked a crime based on people I knew like Abby Hoffman and placed them in a familiar situation (at that point I was walking precincts for McGovern) and off I went without any real guide posts. Three months later, I had a manuscript. A month later, thanks to an old college professor of mine, Ross MacDonald read it and called it a "landmark" in detective fiction, comparing it to Chandler's *The Big Sleep*. Shortly after that, Twentieth Century Fox optioned the book to be directed by that hot young director Marty Scorsese (this, of course, never happened). The novel was translated in a dozen countries. It won prizes in the U. S. and the U. K. I was in fat city. And all by accident.

Actually, I'm being somewhat disingenuous about the outlining. I did make a few cryptic notes to myself that barely took more than a page. Sort of like dots to connect. That was my method then and I've never been able to change it. This has caused me some embarrassment over the years when, as a panelist at mystery conventions, I was asked how I wrote my outlines. I usually looked down and mumbled, hoping that no one heard me, that I really didn't do them. Fortunately, I appeared one time with Tony Hillerman, a true master of the form, who was honest enough to admit in public he didn't make outlines either. From then on, I was saved.

As for the film version, *The Big Fix* took over half a decade to reach the screen. I had already written the sequel novel, *Wild Turkey,* which had been optioned by Warner Brothers. I wrote a script of that novel that the studio allegedly quite liked, and they were about to offer it to a rising young star named Richard Dreyfuss when the head of production changed his mind at the last minute and the offer was never made. Richard and I became friends, however, and it was through his instigation and the help of the legendary film editor Verna Fields that the movie of *The Big Fix* was made at Universal. The studio did not interfere very much in the production, not the way they do now, and the film came out more or less as we designed it. Its faults and successes are pretty much ours.

The book and the film, which already had to treat the Sixties as a receding era, have several differences. The principal one is that in the film Howard Eppis (the Abby Hoffman-like character) is still alive, hiding in plain sight as an adman in an LA suburb, nostalgically singing old Movement songs by the swimming pool. The audience found this amusing, but a couple of years later I learned that it didn't work as well for Abby. I was sitting by myself in a darkened Universal screening room watching a Lubitsch film when the door cracked open. It was Abby, his wife, and their child, America. Although he was underground at the time, a wanted man, he had stopped by the screening room to tell me he thought his characterization in *The Big Fix* was unfair. I didn't bother to tell him how ironic I thought that was given the purpose of his clandestine visit to the studio that day—to sell the movie rights to his own *Steal this Book*.

As with many other cultural phenomena of the decade we call the Sixties (actually 1965-1975), both book and movie created a fair amount of controversy when they came out. They were loved and reviled. Some people called me a communist, others a sexist. Some said I desecrated the detective form, that Moses Wine wasn't sufficiently "hard-boiled." Others wanted to *be* Moses Wine. (One guy, a union organizer, even changed his life because of the book and became a private investigator. Still is.) Some preferred the movie, others thought I sold out my own novel. And so it went. All this seems quaint in the present era when the most important thing about a book is its ranking on Amazon.Com. But then a lot of things have changed and I hope I don't sound too curmudgeonly when I say that not all of them are for the better.

Roger L. Simon
Los Angeles, CA